The Little Wooden Box

Book 2 in the Shady Woods series

J Mercer

Published 2021 / Bare Ink

Printed in the United States of America

Print ISBN: 978-1-7348883-5-5

E-ISBN: 9781734888348

Library of Congress Control Number:TXu002221752

THE LITTLE WOODEN BOX / written by J Mercer

Cover design by Bare Ink

Copy edits by Aurielle Destiche

Contents

Chapter 1

Let It Do Its Thing

Lined up on the counter was an open package of dried seaweed, a paperclip, and an empty, shallow bowl.

I wasn't thinking a paperclip would feel so great going down and looked over at Christian to calm my nerves. He grabbed my hand and threw me a grin as his mom returned from the bathroom with a small jar of shimmering liquid. The silver flecks in her eyes were dull, drained, as she poured the contents of the jar into the bowl. Then she added a few pieces of seaweed.

The siren tears began to pulse and create their own current, churning the seaweed to pieces.

Mrs. Riley waited for it to turn a shiny green before adding the paperclip, at which point the whole thing began to foam. Once the metal was thoroughly devoured, smoke started rising in curls from the center.

She turned to me. "Ready?"

I tried to force an enthusiastic smile, but there was a paperclip in there.

She patted my shoulder and motioned toward the bowl. The liquid had not stopped moving.

"I drink it?" I asked, glancing at Dr. Riley who stood by the sink. Surely a doctor wouldn't let me drink a paperclip.

Mrs. Riley grabbed a towel. "You breathe it in, hon. It'll do the rest. Just lean your head over."

"And don't be alarmed, Grace. Let it do its thing." Christian squeezed my hand as I stepped away from him.

A sure way to alarm someone was to tell them not to be alarmed, but I wanted to see Iara—the watery underbelly of Shady Woods—and the only way to do that was through this bowl. So I squared my shoulders and looked down at the pulsating bowl on the counter.

As I leaned over, I could have sworn it reached for me. Jerking back, I eyed the liquid. "What exactly is it going to do?"

"I think it might be better if you aren't expecting it," Mrs. Riley said.

I didn't like the sound of that. But with a deep breath in and final, unshakeable resolve, I closed my eyes and leaned all the way over. She laid a towel over my head, tenting me in with the microcosm, and I tried to relax with a very unsteady exhale.

The smoke came first, refreshingly cool vapors smelling of sea and sunshine, sending a chill all the way to my lungs. Then something more solid hit my nostrils.

I let out a garbled scream of surprise, and Christian's hand found my back. "It's okay," he whispered. "It won't hurt you."

I opened my eyes but couldn't see much. The towel was lifted from my head. I tried to breathe in through my nose, but there was no longer a pathway there, filled as it was with the thick liquid that was now beginning its descent down my throat. It wasn't painful, just uncomfortable, and, quite frankly, scary as all get out.

It took its time, easing its way at a slower rate than the smoke had before receding from my nose and airways. Like it had disappeared, only I could feel the weight of it in my chest.

I stood up. "What's it doing? I mean, what does it do? How does it let me breathe underwater?"

"It coats the passageway," Mr. Riley explained." And creates little pockets in your lungs so the water can't get through to the tissue where it would do any damage. Then it filters the oxygen out of the water and sends it through."

"Voila! And you now, my dear, can breathe under water!" Mrs. Riley swept the bowl from the counter and dumped the remains in the sink. Not that there was much left.

"I think something's wrong with my eyes," I said. Everything had crisper edges and it was too bright, as if we'd been in the dark and someone had turned on the light. I squinted until it stopped hurting.

"The smoke helps you see like us," Mrs. Riley explained. "Fun, right?"

I scanned the room, wincing when my eyes hit the bright beams of sunlight shooting in through the window. "I didn't know sirens could see like this."

"It'll feel normal when we get there," Christian said. "Rather than cloudy like it usually does when you open your eyes underwater."

"You said all you could do was breathe!" I cried. Christian was a dendrite, like his father and me, but apparently a little more siren than he let on.

He grinned and tugged me toward the basement stairs, down into a dark corner. Though his house was amazing—stone and wood and windows, yet somehow still very sleek—it was built on the foundation of an old lodge, one of the first structures on the lake. This meant the basement was more like a scary old cellar than Stella's. Her house looked old and forgotten on purpose, but the basement let on that it was newer construction.

Tracing his finger over a barely discernible crack in the wall, Christian shoved himself into the cement until a piece of it opened for us. We walked into an empty square closet and he swung the wall back shut. My eyes adjusted to the darkness much more quickly than normal, shadows and outlines explaining so much. From this side, for example, it was clear the chunk of cement Christian had pushed through was actually an ornately carved stone door.

"Ready?" he asked.

"Ready."

With the crank of a rusty wheel, water started to spill in at the edge of the ceiling. It poured down the wall and swirled around my bare feet.

As it reached my waist, I realized this was it. It was going to fill this little room, and we weren't going to stop it. I clung to Christian when it neared my chest, stood on my tiptoes as it covered my shoulders, and squeezed my eyes shut as it rose over my face.

Don't hold your breath, he instructed, his voice filling my head as the water swallowed us. *Just breathe like normal.*

I tried, but my body refused, which resulted in a lot of coughing and sputtering.

Relax.

He was breathing effortlessly. If he could, I could too. Supposedly.

Focusing on the easy swishing into and out of his nose, I took a deep breath in. The water was warm, and the heat spread to my lungs, but when I exhaled, the warmth disappeared. I missed it, wanted it, so I inhaled again.

With a smile, I loosened the life or death hold I had on him. *That's not uncomfortable.*

No, it's not. Are you ready for more?

More what? What happens next?

He grinned, then worked a lever situated below the wheel. The floor slid out from under us.

We fell with the water, like we were being flushed down a slide. Where it turned, we turned. Where it twisted, we twisted. Where it sped, we sped. And it sped just about the whole way, slowing only at the end, where it leveled off and deposited us into another little room, not unlike the last, where Christian helped me to my feet.

There were wheels on both walls in this room, the first to close a sliding door over the tube behind us, and the second to open a door in front of us.

Reaching for my hand, he led me in a strange walking swim down a slanted hall. The only light emanated weakly from round orbs along the wall, and the floor was flat. I wasn't sure I'd ever felt anything so smooth.

There were a few small archways leading to what I assumed were bedrooms, but we didn't stop until the end of the hall where the space opened up on its own. The furniture was stone—a round squatty ball, a flat square with no sharp edges, a smooth concaved cup—while a vase with softly swaying foliage sat on the end table. Green curtains flowed gently on the glassless windows, drawings were etched into the stone wall itself, and books lined a few carved out cubbies.

How are there books down here?

Pulling out the largest one, he handed it to me. *Sirens had books before humans were even humans.*

The spine was essentially a narrow pouch of stones, probably to weigh it down, and the pages were thin, nearly transparent. *What's it made of?*

Octopus, whale, or shark skin.

I ran my fingers down the ink.

From a squid, tattooed on, he explained, as if he could read my thoughts. But he couldn't. It didn't work like that. A dendrite could only send, not take. *The skin is shaved to produce multiple copies. Not quite as efficient as a printing press, but it works.*

The writing was on one side of each page, the ink showing through to leave a mirrored copy on the back. Definitely not English.

He flipped it closed to run his finger along the title as he translated: *The Complete Dictionary of Tear Formulas.*

I slid it back in place and ran my fingers across the spines of the rest of them, marveling over the uniqueness of each, their sizes and shapes entirely dependent on the particular pebbles or rocks that held them together.

Kind of magical, right?

More than kind of, I replied.

That's it for in here, he said. *The houses are simple: one gathering room and some sleeping rooms. No kitchen, no fancy mudroom, no offices.*

He led me out the front opening and onto a pebbled path lined with what could have been tufts of prairie grass. As the waves from our movement reached the tufts, they wafted slowly in the other direction.

At the end of the walkway, I turned back for a better view of the neighboring houses. All long and thin and made of rock, they were nestled against a severe drop in the lake's floor.

The sunlight streamed in from above, obscured and filtered by the depth of the water. I couldn't see anything up there, couldn't tell if what looked like clouds were people or boats or ducks—couldn't tell how deep we were, except that we were pretty darn deep.

We came to a squat stone wall, and Christian pointed over it to the backs of the little buildings on the other side. He explained that the town itself was made up of concentric circles, as if someone drew a huge circle on the lake bottom to make the path we were now on, then the wall, then another path, a ring of small shops and businesses, and in the very center, a park. As we came to a break in the wall, he laced his fingers through mine and led me through an alley between two of the stores to the park. This town circle, let's call it, held benches, more greenery, a statue, and a fountain.

A fountain?

I went straight for it. Large rocks surrounded the base, and water rushed up but never came down. An endless upward movement.

Christian laced his fingers through mine and pulled me toward a bench. Was there a place on land even remotely comparable?

I'd come back anytime, I announced.

Well, you can decide that after we get out.

Is that the uncomfortable part?

That's the uncomfortable part.

What about for you? What's it like for you?

Uncomfortable.

Well, maybe we should get it over with then.

If I had my way I'd keep you down here forever. He ran his fingers through my hair, which was currently floating around me from the most recent turn of my head, then pulled me closer to him.

Is this about your dream? I asked. He turned his head away in response.

I'd come to find out that Christian was something of a crystal ball. He had dreams like anyone else, but some of his came true. So far just little things he told me about in the morning that ended up actually happening by the end of the week.

Last night, though, he'd dreamt I was bitten by a wolf who stole me away to the moon where Christian couldn't reach me.

You can't be sure it means anything, I pointed out for the umpteenth time. *Maybe it was just a normal dream.*

It was not a normal dream.

Maybe it's not literal.

They're always literal.

There's nothing literal about me ending up on the moon.

He still wouldn't look at me, so I watched the sirens on the path in front of us. Some had stones twined through their hair, which held it down so it didn't float everywhere and get in their face, while some looked to be using normal hair ties. The old and the new, I imagined, just like what they wore. Some had nothing but hair covering their torsos, others had bikini or tube tops on, and one woman was wrapped in linen, except it probably wasn't linen. It was probably some lake plant or the skin of some fish or something else like that they could find down here. Their hair, of course, was always thick and luscious so it covered most of what needed covering, not that they seemed too concerned about it, and their tails were bright and shiny, reflecting the few rays of light that managed to reach all the way down here.

The children had hair nearly as long as their mothers, which meant they were often dragging it along behind them, and the whole mood was lazy and slow. But in a good way, as if they were taking their time, enjoying the moment, rather than rushing through to their final destination.

My final destination was not the moon. That was an impossibility. I glanced over at Christian. His brow was furrowed, and he was watching the fountain, except also clearly not watching it. Still absorbed in his dream. I wrapped my arms around him from the side, since we sat next to each other on the bench, then rested my head against his shoulder.

I'm not going anywhere, I promised.

He relaxed a little and turned his head to let my hair dance across his face.

The rest of our time there felt like some sort of romantic movie, and when it was time to leave, we swam up rather than go back through the house. Christian thought the floating, flying kind of feeling you got when you watched a city grow smaller below you was an experience not to miss.

Breaking the surface was an assault to my senses, a shocking contrast to the hushed quiet of Iara. I felt so aware, so alive, everything sharpened without the muting effect of the water.

When it started to fade, I rubbed at my eyes, feeling desperate for a pair of glasses. Then I started coughing.

Try to hold it in until we get to shore.

Try to hold what in?

The coughing. Trust me.

So I did. Or I tried. I lost it a few times, but managed to reach his dock just fine. Pulling ourselves up past the lily pads, we collapsed on the smooth wood.

Then I let it out, the cough. Christian did too. He was on all fours, head hanging over the pier, so I followed his lead. It started as a soft tickle in my throat, innocent enough until the tickle ripped violently through me, until the water came pouring out in gushes, through our mouths and noses.

Ew, I commented.

I know.

When that was finished, my lungs seemed to convulse, or ripple, or shake. Christian collapsed, but my body was still trying to rid itself of something. Finally, with one effective jerk, the tear mixture came pouring back out of me. Through my mouth and through my nose, it flew into the water, landing with a plunk.

I dropped to the warmth of the dock as chills raced through me. I was well aware that the sun was hot, that the wood beneath me was hot, that even my skin was hot, but the cold came from inside and I couldn't shake it. I pressed my face against the pier and spread my arms out to soak it up.

Christian crawled over and draped a toasty arm over my back. He lined his body up against mine, and I felt him like a fire.

This is what I was talking about, he noted. *Uncomfortable.*

"Are you warm?" My teeth were chattering.

"Yeah, it's from the tear formula that you're cold. Or lack of, now."

"So how does your body do it?" I motioned to where my silver glob had dropped. "Without the formula?"

"We're not sure exactly. My Dad thinks the shield that the tears create in you is in me all the time. That it comes and goes as it needs to. He thinks the lung tissue rejects it once it senses the air, once the water's gone. I can feel it, like you can, just nothing ends up coming out."

"Is that what siren lungs are like?"

"No, they have one lung for water and one for air. Their body just knows."

"Of course it does," I muttered.

No violence or greed inherent in their society. No unsightly body hair. Just beauty and charm and a body that knows where it is and how to react. Instinct.

What I wouldn't give for a little instinct—and, as a double bonus, to never have to shave again.

Chapter 2

Score One For Flattery

My palms were sweaty, and I was biting my lower lip, trying not to fidget as Christian pulled open the door to Al's. We were hanging out with his friends for the first time tonight. Friends who did not like me.

In fact, Sofia and Emily didn't like me so much that they had refused to come. And Jeremy, who liked me enough at least, wouldn't be there because he had a date. That left Aster and Kevin, who weren't there yet, so we found a booth, and I opened a menu. Al's was a burger joint with a nostalgic kind of vibe, even though it had been newly rebuilt after the fires last fall. Al had rebuilt it exactly as it had been, with huge corner booths, metal padded chairs at the tables, and walls decorated with posters of vampire and werewolf movies.

My friend Stella liked to bug Al about not representing the sirens, but he kept telling her he wasn't about sappy love stories. He'd just wave a hand at her and walk away, yelling over his shoulder, "Let me know when the next siren horror film is released!"

His very thin burgers were topped with pats of butter and sandwiched between crispy buns, and his custard (a creamy, thick ice cream that sat somewhere between hard packed and soft serve)could cool you down to your toes on a hot summer day.

This would be one of the last of those, as school started up next week. Precisely why I figured it was time to really meet Christian's friends. Christian and I had started slow at first, considering he and Sofia had hardly been over when we began. Over the summer, avoiding them had also been easy enough, but now, going back to school...

The door chimed as Aster and Kevin arrived, and Aster offered me what might have been the first genuine smile I'd seen from her.

She was in jean shorts and a bright red t-shirt, with dainty gold necklaces strung around her neck. I knew she was a werewolf, Native American, and also maybe the most intimidating person I'd ever met. Not in a bad way, like Sofia, but in a I-have-my-crap-together-and-am-more-impressive-than-you-could-even-imagine kind of way.

Christian grinned as Aster slid into the booth, and Kevin flopped down after her. I smiled, but couldn't force out any words. This was Sofia's best friend. One of the triad. So I was assuming she hated me at least a little bit. That's what friends did for each other, right?

"Sorry I'm such a mess." She rolled her eyes. "My mom had me cleaning all day. We hardly made it."

"You look amazing, as usual." This spilled out of me before I had time to filter.

She beamed. "I like you already."

Well, score one for flattery.

"Besides,"—I sighed—"my hair is *always* a mess. "What I wouldn't give for smooth, pretty hair.

"Please, your hair is perfectly imperfect." She waved her hand. "Like you just stepped off the beach wherever it is you're from."

Chicago, so the beaches weren't much different from the ones around here. No salty ocean air, but sure.

Kevin nodded at me, and I nodded back. He was a blond, brown-eyed siren, and where most people would come off as ill-mannered and bloated the way he was sprawled in the booth like a lazy walrus, he looked like he was posing for an artist.

I sighed, feeling sickeningly regular among the beauty around me. They could be models, each of them. What was I doing here? I was so obviously normal, nothing but a misplaced dendrite, born into a normal world and only recently dropped down into this one. Maybe if I'd been born here, instead of just showing up last year, maybe then Christian's friends wouldn't be so hard on me.

No. That was wishful thinking. They were pretty hard on everybody.

Christian looked over at the sound of my heavy exhale and pulled my hand to his lap so he could play with my fingers.

Aster was coiling her hair around her pinky and studying the menu, while Kevin's eyes roamed the room like he was already bored.

"We went to Iara today," Christian said.

Aster's head shot up at this, and a lazy smile spread on Kevin's face.

"I love Iara!" She grinned at me as if we shared a secret. "We should all go down there sometime. I always wanted to do that with Sofia and Christian, but she never liked the idea."

"Really?" I asked. "Why not?"

"Sofia doesn't do what Sofia doesn't want to do," Kevin replied.

"She says vampires were not meant for water," Christian added. "Probably thought she'd be lowering herself."

Aster studied me, then whispered across the table, "He's so much happier with you."

I blinked and chewed a little of the skin on the inside of my lip. Could it really be this easy, winning them over?

"That's because he is," Kevin said, in what I was gathering was his regular monotone. "Sofia can be a royal pain in the butt."

Aster gave him a warning look. "Can we please not talk about our friend like that?"

He shrugged. "You started it."

"Okay," Christian patted my hand and stood up. *Now that I feel comfortable enough to leave you,* "I'll go order for us."

Kevin joined him, and they walked up to the counter.

Aster crossed her arms on the table and leaned into them. "Speaking of friends, I saw Riah at the last full moon."

Like all werewolves, Riah and Aster transformed wild at the full moon. Ruled by animal instinct and void of human thought and self-control, they hunted whatever live meat they came across. Shady Woods wolves avoided human targets by escaping to the deepest wilderness so they'd only find animals and not people.

"Quetico looks amazing," I said, thinking of the pictures I saw of Riah's recent trip.

"Quetico *is* amazing," she confirmed. "We ran into Riah and his family on our way in and ended up camping together."

"You do that?"

"Sometimes." She shrugged. "Anyway, Riah was *cranky*. And a total mess after."

"Are you usually not a mess?"

"Let's just say it seemed like he was looking for a fight. It happens. I can't say I've never had a month like that. Anyway, you should check up on him. Sometimes us wolves aren't so great about expressing our feelings. Maybe we forget everyone can't smell us like we can smell them."

And that's when I wanted to pound my forehead against the table, because how had I forgotten? All my nerves and she could smell them. Instead, I slid my hands over my face with a groan. How embarrassing.

Aster laughed. "Don't worry. I know everyone's intimidated by me. You smell braver than most, to be honest."

Christian and Kevin returned to the table in time to hear that, and Kevin asked, "She smells good, then?"

Aster nodded with a smile.

Kevin nodded at me, looking more engaged than I'd seen him yet. "I'm impressed."

What are they talking about? I asked Christian.

Sofia and Emily might not be friendly, but Aster actually is. She just can't stand the smell of everyone's reaction to her, and the more she talks to people, the worse it usually gets, not better. I don't know why. It's not like she's the mean one.

I looked at him, wondering if he realized his ex-girlfriend *was* the mean one.

Al's son, who was on the basketball team with Christian and Kevin, came by to drop our food. No words were exchanged, but they all bumped fists before he left the table to go back to work.

Aster rolled her eyes to me and mouthed, "Boys."

Do they bump chests too? I asked, before realizing I hadn't been invited into her head. My face froze for a minute, but hers lit up. She held a hand out to me, and we pretended we had some secret long handshake, except we didn't and it was a hot mess, so we were laughing by the end.

Kevin looked at us like we were crazy. "What are they doing?"

"Making fun of us," Christian answered.

We ate our food through scattered, less awkward conversation, and I finally started to relax. When Kevin finished his raw cod, he reached over to take a bite out of Aster's burger. It was sitting unattended on her plate, waiting for her to finish the towering raw beef cone she'd started with.

She slapped his hand. "No." Then she pointed her finger at Christian. "Don't you get any ideas, either."

I laughed.

"What?" She looked at me, innocent as an angel. "You have to watch your food around these two, seriously."

She could eat as much as Riah and that was saying something. Wolves definitely had the biggest appetite of all of us. She even insisted on dessert. Four of them to share, and every minute she had us sending the dish in front of us over to the next person. It didn't seem like a new thing to them, but like I was being initiated.

So one meal and we were the kind of friends who swapped spit. I decided that was a really good sign as Sofia and Emily walked in, boyfriends trailing behind them. Sofia found me immediately, and when she did, a scowl brightened her face.

Yes, she was so awful that a scowl was an improvement on her baseline facial expression. I don't know what Christian ever saw in her. He noticed them next, then Aster, who twisted in her seat and threw up a little wave while muttering under her breath, "This should be interesting."

Turning back to our desserts, she called for us to switch again.

I slid the mint Oreo shake across the table, then swirled the spoon around in the melting root beer float glass. The conversation continued as it had before, but I kept one eye on the person who was about to ruin my night.

I was with Sofia's ex-boyfriend and best friend. There was no hope whatsoever that she'd leave us alone.

The four of them found a table, and then Sofia and Emily got up to head our way. We grew quiet, one by one, as they approached.

They were carbon copies of each other, with long, dark hair and pale skin that looked like it had never seen the sun. Vampires were mostly laid back and somewhat unemotional, though I wouldn't say that of these two. The ones living in Shady Woods drank two large glasses of blood a day, twice as much as a wild vampire. It was how we kept them happily sated so their instinct to drink from fresh bodies was tempered.

Sofia and Emily were also tall and thin. This was common, if not a rule, for vampires. They looked quite intimidating as a team, though Sofia alone would have done it for me. Even on her best days she made me squirm with unease.

"Hi." Aster smiled, as if there was nothing unusual about the situation. These were, after all, her best friends.

"Hi," Sofia clipped, scanning everyone's faces but mine. She did not look my way. Emily, however, was trying to stare me down.

"Come sit with us," Sofia said to Aster. "Salvage the rest of your evening."

"Oh, I..."

You can go, I told her, not wanting to get in the middle. *I understand.*

"No," she said. "I'm good. I think we'll stay here."

Sofia leaned back in disbelief, and Emily laughed. "You poor thing, you don't need to feel guilty. Right, Sofia? She doesn't need to feel guilty. Just come on, already."

"You were invited and chose not to come," Christian said. "So leave us alone."

Sofia's head jerked toward him. "You don't own her, Christian. She'll do what she wants."

"You don't own her either," he snapped." And she just told you what she wanted."

"Aster!" Sofia cried.

"What? What do you want me to say?"

"I want you to say you'd rather eat her than sit here for one more minute." With this, Sofia looked at me, as if to say 'yes, in fact, I did just speak of eating you. Have a problem with that?'

For the record, I did have a problem with that. It never failed to escape my attention that I was highly edible among the world of above-normals.

"Always so pleasant." I smiled. "That's what I love most about you."

"Shut up, Grace, or I'll put my fist in your mouth and do it for you."

"Put your fist in my mouth and I'll put a head of garlic in yours," I snapped.

Sofia gasped and stepped back. Emily mirrored her reaction, a moment behind. A vampire would die if they ingested garlic, but I didn't think this was so out of line considering she was just talking about eating me.

"I'm bored," Kevin said. "Can you finish up this catfight please?" He began to strum his fingertips on the table, directing a look toward me.

It wasn't pleasant. It wasn't a reassuring, I'm-on-your-side look.

I shrank back into the seat and into Christian, who squeezed his arm around me.

"Are you going to let her talk to me that way?!" Sofia hissed at Aster.

Aster pushed at Kevin to move him out of the booth so she could get free. "I can't control her. What would you have me do?"

"Are we going?" Kevin asked, as she stood up next to him.

"No, you stay. I'll be right back." And she pulled the two girls by their elbows back to their boyfriends.

"You could maybe not mess with them," Kevin suggested.

I opened my mouth to defend myself but didn't know what to say. Wasn't it clear I hadn't been the one to start the messing?

"Honestly?" Christian responded for me.

"Yeah, yeah. But don't you think this is hard enough on Aster as it is? Sofia already feels like she's been betrayed and then to put her on the spot like that?" Kevin nodded toward the other table where a heated conversation was taking place.

"Grace didn't put anyone on the spot. Sofia was the one who came over here and put Aster on the spot. Don't defend her." Christian was starting to get worked up, and I was starting to feel horrible.

I grimaced. "I'm sorry."

"No, you're not!" Christian turned to me. "All you did was defend yourself!"

Kevin tilted his head in agreement before quickly going back to being bored. Aster came back, pushing Kevin over to slide in next to him.

"And?" Kevin asked.

"It's fine. She's over it. Let's talk about something else." But it seemed she was having a hard time looking at me.

"She doesn't get over things," Christian muttered.

"What'd you say to her?" Kevin asked.

"I told her what she wanted to hear." Yes, she was definitely having a hard time looking at me. "I told her it was rude to expect us to bail at the snap of her fingers. That she needed to give us a minute. Or thirty."

"So you told her you didn't like my new girlfriend." Christian's voice was controlled but angry.

"I did not say that. I didn't say anything bad, I just…"She turned to me. "I'm sorry. I like you a lot, really. You two are really cute together—"

I put up my hand to cut her off. It felt like she was overdoing it out of guilt. "It's okay." I was disappointed but not mad. Had I really expected her to choose me? It would've been nice but unrealistic. She'd only met me, really, that very night.

"I just wanted her to calm down." She was pleading with us both. "She's upset, and I know you have every right to be upset too, but—"

"She comes first. We get it." Christian was definitely bitter.

"We should go," I said. "I don't want you to have to be in the middle. "The night had been ruined anyway. Sofia made sure of that.

"I didn't mean it, what I told her. I'm so sorry."

"Are you?" Christian challenged. "Because we all know you've had your moments, just like Sofia."

"Hey! Uncalled for!" Kevin cried, but Aster took it. She nodded.

"That's fair, Chris. But then you also know that if I didn't like Grace, we'd be long gone from this table, and I wouldn't be feeling bad about it."

"How big of you," Christian said, standing to leave.

"Okay, can that please be enough now?" I asked him. Then I turned back to Aster, who looked tortured and small in the big booth. "He'll get over it, and I'm okay. Don't worry about it."

She smiled sadly, and offered me her hand. Christian was already at the front door, but I didn't hurry. I took it, and we made another lame attempt at a ridiculously long handshake.

Then I walked away.

"You shouldn't have let her off so easy," Christian grumbled as I joined him outside.

"Are you feeling protective?" I teased, snaking my arm around his waist and squeezing him tight.

"Really, Grace, that was awful."

"I would've done the same thing if Stella or Charlie felt like I was with the enemy." I would have. I wouldn't have been proud of it, but friends came first. In fact, I'd like to believe I wouldn't even be with the enemy in the first place.

I kissed him, to convince him, and sort of hoped Sofia could see us through the glass front wall of Al's. We were standing in the dark, but we were there, and we were happy.

It was more than I could say for her.

Chapter 3

What's So Stupid About an Eyeball?

Stella pulled her long, strawberry-blond hair into a ponytail and folded herself onto Ethan's lap, taking the little wooden box out of his hands and setting it on the coffee table in his basement.

Ethan was always futzing with the box, tossing it in the air or dropping it from one hand to the other like a hot potato. It drove her nuts.

"Still no luck getting it open?" I was sitting next to Riah, my dog sprawled on his lap.

"I'm about to take a hammer to it," Ethan muttered.

"No way," Riah said. "That would be a travesty."

I agreed; it was a work of art. Intricate carvings were scattered across the light wood: a vampire's profile on the front, fangs protruding, and a werewolf howling at the moon on the lid. A brain spread across the back, curling around the edge, and two sirens were superimposed on top of one another on the bottom, one with legs under one with a tail.

"Strange that it so obviously belongs to an abnormal," I said.

"That's what's got me so obsessed with it." Ethan was serious about this, though his faint expression was self-mocking.

I turned it over in my hand. Another side held scribbles and designs and pictures I couldn't decipher, along with trees and stars and wavy lines we'd decided were supposed to depict the sea. I tried to slide my fingernail under the dark pewter clasp, but there was no wiggle room, then set it back on the table.

"So what's in the box?" Stella asked, because this had become a game.

"Jewelry," I guessed. "Diamonds."

"That doesn't make any sense," Riah said. "Why would all that abnormal garbage be on there if it was just a jewelry box?"

"It could be a jewelry box carved for an abnormal," I pointed out.

"I think it's an eyeball," Stella said.

"An eyeball?" Riah scratched his arm and then his neck.

She shrugged. "Something gory. You know, like the eyeball of the owner's first human victim."

Ethan snorted. "No one in Shady Woods has ever had a human victim."

Riah started to itch again, scraping at his skin so hard it sounded like it might come off. "Does this dog have fleas?"

"No." I gave him a look. "And be careful, you're leaving marks."

"I can't help it. I itch." He pushed Zeus off him and started scratching at his neck with both hands. "Seriously, give him a bath or something."

"What's so stupid about an eyeball?" Stella demanded.

"I didn't say it was stupid," Ethan replied.

She raised her eyebrows. "I could tell you thought it was stupid by the tone of your voice."

"I have to get away from him," Riah said, standing to bound up the stairs.

The three of us looked at each other. Ethan shrugged. Zeus was already following Riah, and since Riah was trying to get away from him, I ran after, catching up with them in the front yard.

"Where're you going?"

"Home." His left hand was still working at his neck.

"I've barely seen you lately."

"Fine, but keep that dog away from me."

"You love that dog," I pointed out.

"Not today."

I directed Zeus to the backyard and met Riah in our kitchen. "Better?" I asked, as he rummaged in our fridge.

"Yes." He straightened. "Your mom probably has some designated use for that ground beef, huh?"

"Probably. If there's bacon left, you can have that."

I settled on a stool at the counter as he slapped the package of bacon between us, peeling away a piece and tilting his head back to drop it in his mouth.

I barely shivered at all. "So, where've you been?"

"Where've you been?" he countered, watching me while he ate two more pieces.

"Aster said she saw you at the last full moon, that you were all sulky and came back a mess, like you were looking for a fight."

He snorted. "Aster told you? She your new best friend now?"

I made a face. A 'shut up' face.

He finished off the last three pieces of bacon in silence, threw the wrapper away, washed his hands, and scratched once more at his neck, where the red marks were finally starting to fade.

"So you're hanging out with Aster now?" But his tone had changed. It was almost back to normal, conversational and in-terested.

"A little. Her and Kevin and Jeremy and whoever Jeremy brings with." I told him about the first night at Al's. He busted out laughing when I told him what I'd said to Sofia. "But Aster's cool. I like her; we'd be friends. I mean, real friends, if it weren't for Sofia."

"She was my first kiss," he admitted.

"When? I want details!"

"At recess, maybe seventh grade. No tongue or anything, just a peck. I think we'd been going out for three weeks or something.

That was forever back then. Anyway, she broke up with me for Jeremy."

"Jeremy and Aster were together?"

"In seventh grade, and I think again in eighth."

"No way!"

He rested his hip against the counter. "Who was your first kiss?"

"Matteo, in sixth. But it was the whole 'kiss and run' kind of thing."

"After I kissed Aster, I didn't leave her side. It was pathetic, really. That's probably why she broke up with me."

"That's cute, you and Aster. Who'd have thought?"

Riah rolled his eyes. "That doesn't even count anymore, seventh grade."

I traced the pattern on the counter with my fingertip for a moment, thinking about seventh grade and my normal childhood. He was right. It didn't even count anymore.

When I looked up, he was watching me. "Has it really been three weeks since I've seen you?" I asked. We used to see each other every single day.

"About."

"I'm sorry." Riah had become my best friend over the last year, and I'd vowed not to forget about him, even though I was distracted with Christian. I guess I hadn't done a very good job.

He shrugged, but a frown tugged at his mouth. "No worries, I get it."

A soft howl from Zeus drifted in through the window. I felt it too, and deep. "He misses you," I said.

Riah snorted. "Don't make me feel bad."

"We could give him a bath and take him on a walk." A long one, around town and through the woods, maybe without my phone so I wouldn't be distracted by Christian. "One of those things—the bath or just being outside—has to help the itching more than Ethan's stinky basement."

He grinned and went to let Zeus inside.

Chapter 4

I'm Sure It's Nothing

"So we were all in the window—"

"Please clarify," I interrupted. We were on our way to school. Christian had not only gotten a driver's license in mid-September but also a car. On top of that, he went out of his way to pick me up. I didn't even have to ask.

"The window at the General Store."

"Oh, right." There was a room inside the general store that you got to through a window in the back alley. Stella had told me about it last year. All the businesses in town kept their weird, abnormal stuff hidden in some way or another, in case a normal happened by.

"So we were all in the window—"

"Who's all?"

"You, me, Stella, Ethan, and Riah."

"Ok." I nodded for him to continue.

"There was a wall of keys, a whole wall." Christian turned to me, "They don't have a wall of keys. They've never had a wall of keys," then back to the road. "But we were there and taking them off one by one, chewing on them and putting them back. Isn't that weird?"

"Very."

"I don't know what we were expecting to find, but the chewing seemed important. What would we do with a chewable key?"

"Chew it?"

"I like that you find my dreams amusing."

I studied him.

"I'm serious. Sofia was always pressing me to tell her exactly what they meant, like I could unlock the secrets to the universe."

"Well, I don't think they're a joke," I assured him, as he turned into the school parking lot." Do you think this means I'll finally get to see the window?"

"I'll take you to the window any time you want," he said, pulling into a spot.

I swung open the door, letting all the noise in: honks of greeting, shouts for people to wait up, and all-around general chaos.

There was no chaos in my first class, even though Sofia and Emily were Mrs. Smith's favorites. They sat in the front, which meant it was impossible for them to stare me down. Plus, I could scowl at the back of their heads all I wanted or ignore them for the entire hour, and they had nothing to say about it.

Natural history meant we'd be learning how each of us came to be, how we lived in the early years, and why we transitioned to our way of life today. We'd started with the sirens, had already been over their diet and how they lived in traveling schools for hundreds of years until the first king took rule and shifted their thinking.

"The sirens fell for a king in the first place," Mrs. Smith was saying, "because of all the deaths they were facing. They'd stumbled upon humans…"—pulling down the map, she tapped the places listed in our text as the first meeting points—"…and realized how easily their bodies adjusted to land. This will be on the exam, Cynthia." Her heels clicked their way to the desk of a girl in the third row. "The discoveries of the Great Discoverers were land and legs. Write that down at the very least, will you?"

She waited while Cynthia pulled out a pen and started scribbling, then moved back up to perch on her desk. "When word got out, many sirens wanted to experience it themselves, but humans are fearful, wary, and distrustful. Sirens were unknown, and if tail morphing was witnessed, it most often resulted in the siren being attacked, beaten, and left for dead. Humans thought of them as animals—fish, ocean mammals—and some considered them a delicacy. As you can imagine, the sirens learned to be cautious. They also learned they had some semblance of control over the humans.

"Sirens, as you know, can communicate with sea creatures. Their underwater language is heard and understood, though not spoken, by most of the larger, more intelligent creatures underwater. But siren charm also helps a siren control the lesser fish, those that don't understand them. Now, let's remember for a moment that to a siren, proceeding cautiously is to proceed slowly, easing great charm. This is natural for them. They don't need to think about it as they do it. So the more cautious they became on land, the more they found their charm worked on humans too. Some tried to live on land completely, but this didn't provide enough moisture. When they began spending their days on land and nights in the water, new illnesses began to hit the siren population. Many died. It seemed almost everyone who came in contact with the diseased grew ill themselves, and most of them never recovered."

Scanning ahead in my book, I read about King Thedorius. He was distraught with the suffering of his people and didn't know what to do about it. None of the medical help they were getting on land was having any effect, and none of the traditional siren cures were doing anything either. He sent word to gather all the sirens together. This was a crisis that needed action, blah, blah, blah.

I jumped to the last paragraph. It was now known as The Great Gathering of King Thedorius. They loved him, and his ideas, and decided to give him absolute power to fix things.

"Please read the chapters on King Thedorius for homework. We'll talk about him the next few days, and I want you to be willing and able to discuss." Mrs. Smith tapped the textbook that was on her desk with a long, painted fingernail. This seemed to cue the bell.

Spanish with Riah was next. Then chemistry with Aster, English with Stella, and lunch.

I sat down next to Christian at our lunch table, while Ethan landed next to Stella. As soon as Riah sat on my other side, Stella asked if we'd heard about Addison Jacobs.

"Doesn't she live by you?" she asked Riah.

He nodded, while the rest of us shook our heads. No, we hadn't heard about her. Except Christian wasn't shaking his head. I elbowed him.

"I'm not supposed to gossip about my dad's patients," he mumbled.

"She's out sick today, but everyone's saying she died." Stella said this nonchalantly, as if she wasn't goading him, but how could he let that be what everyone was saying, if it weren't true?

"That's crap," Christian muttered, and Stella winked at me. "She was attacked last night by that stretch of woods in her neighborhood. She's in stable condition, all hooked up and under transformation."

"Under transformation?" I echoed. "What does that mean?"

"It means she was bit by a vampire," Christian grumbled. "And I shouldn't have said anything."

"That's not supposed to happen here!" I cried, which pulled everyone's attention to me. I lowered my voice and hissed, "I thought that wasn't supposed to happen here."

"It hasn't happened in fifty-three years," Riah said.

"It was Reilly's uncle fifty-three years ago," Ethan said. "And probably Reilly now."

Nehemiah, Reilly, and Preston were always getting blamed for everything. Last year, everyone thought they were burning up the town. Only, it hadn't been them. Just because they ran around town till all hours of the night and liked to sneak out into the normal world did not mean they were dangerous.

"Why would anyone do that?" I asked.

"To find out how good it really tastes," Ethan muttered, carefully not looking in my direction. "Or so they say. That it tastes good. Really good. Amazing."

I raised an eyebrow.

"I would never, though. None of us would."

"Well, someone did."

"I'm sure it's nothing." Stella reached over Christian for my hand. Mine, because again I was the weakest link.

Dendrite blood, uncontaminated by any other abnormal ancestor, was as good as human blood when it came down to it. Plenty abnormals respected us as "like them" because of what we could do with our brains, but our bodies were closest to a human's.

This was my life, and I'd accepted it. But being changed into a vampire? There would be nothing worse. I'd never be able to go back to the normal world. Even a werewolf could manage in Chicago, as long as they got far away on the full moon, but as a vampire, my choice to live normal or abnormal would be taken away.

"I'm sure it was a one-time thing, Grace," Riah said, cued into my thoughts with his sense of smell alone.

"What happened to Reilly's uncle?" I asked.

"Nothing," Ethan replied. "He only did it once, and if I remember right, there was consent involved in that one."

I blinked.

"Sorry I brought it up." Stella wilted a little, then perked up. "What do you think's in that little wooden box?"

Her go-to distraction. I smiled.

"I think it's a box of fingernails," she said. "Did you hear about that guy that kept a collection of his own fingernail clippings? They found a drawer of them when he died."

"Maybe it's a finger," Riah offered. "Or a toe."

"That's disgusting," Christian said. "Why can't it be something sweet, like someone's first kiss?"

"Ooh!" Stella raised her hand, like she was eight and begging to be called on. "Or someone's lips!"

Riah raised an eyebrow at her. "When did you get so morbid?"

"If only there was a key," Ethan grumbled.

I was instantly alert. "We should go to the window! Christian had this dream." I turned to him and found his eyes wide.

Oops. Was I not supposed to tell anyone about the dreams? I pressed my lips together and waited for permission to continue.

He closed his eyes. *Go ahead.*

"We all went to the window and there was a wall of keys. Maybe it's there."

"There's no wall of keys in the window," Stella pointed out.

"That's what I told her," Christian said.

"But they do have a lost and found! Maybe the key's in the lost and found!" Ethan slammed a palm on the table, causing Stella's empty water bottles to jump. "You guys! People bring them stuff from all over town! Why haven't I thought of this sooner?"

We aren't going to find anything, Christian warned me. *We didn't find anything in the dream.*

Tell him that then.

No.

Why not?

Because they'll think I believe my dreams come true, and that's corny.

I leaned into him, because it was cute that he cared what my friends thought of him, as much as me caring what his friends thought of me. *But your dreams do come true.*

"Who's in?" Ethan was squirmy, which was saying something. "I'm going right after school."

"I'm in," I said. "I need to see this window."

"What happens if you're bit by a vampire?" I asked Riah as we sat down in geometry.

"If you're bit by a vampire, you turn into a vampire."

I rolled my eyes at him. "Thank you for the specifics."

"You get a high fever and sweat it out for days," Aster said from my other side. "And you want blood, lots and lots of blood. They probably have her locked up somewhere so she doesn't hurt anyone."

This had been an interesting development, the two of them on either side of me. Particularly because Riah thought Aster was a snob, and Aster thought Riah was gloomy. Not to mention, Riah didn't think any friend of Sofia's could be a friend of mine, and Aster thought Riah was a nosy pain in the butt.

I would have thought he was a pain in the butt too, if he needled me the way he always needled her. They talked over each other, as if the other wasn't there, and it was difficult to keep up with both of them. I wasn't sure how I was going to last the year without going insane.

"What about her skills?" I asked. "Is she not a dendrite any-more?"

"You keep your brain, but your body changes," Riah said. "So she'll be able to communicate like you, plus be fast and indestructible. And want blood."

"What about her...shape?" I asked.

"You're worried about her looks?"

Aster patted her hair with a wink. "As any good friend would be."

I rolled my eyes. "Not like that. I mean, she's not tall."

Aster smirked. "I hear you say she's not tall and know you mean she's not skinny."

I shifted uncomfortably in my seat. Every body was beautiful, but I'd never seen a vampire who wasn't thin.

Not that I'd seen a vast majority of them or anything.

"She'll grow," Riah said. "Don't worry."

The bell rang, and though class went on, my brain was stuck, trying to imagine what I'd look like if I were a vampire.

Christian and Ethan could tell I was off during gym, and as we walked to skills, Christian shook the hand of mine he was holding. "You okay?"

"I'm fine. Better than fine. Super great." At least, I wanted to be.

He gave me a funny look but dropped it. I focused as best I could on Mr. Turner. We were working on sending pictures. This was a little different than having a conversation, and I hadn't figured out what it would be useful for. The hardest part was not blurting out the word. I was so used to speaking in my head but with pictures you had to be careful not to.

As usual, we'd started with holding hands and facing each other but were now on to avoiding both eye contact and touch. So I waited like that, stealing glimpses of Christian out of the corner of my eye, until his first picture came. It was always a heart, *his* heart he liked to specify, but it looked different every day.

Enough already with the hearts, I told him. *You've got to be more creative than that.*

He pouted. *You don't like my hearts?*

Letting out a dramatic sigh, I sent him one of my own: a pulsating, dripping with blood, honest-to-goodness heart. As if I'd ripped it from my chest.

He snorted. *A true romantic you are.*

You don't like it? It's my very own.

His frown faded as our eyes met. *I do like it. Of course I do.*

I rested my head on my desk. The effort that one picture took had prompted a headache. My brain was fried. Even though I could effortlessly speak to a whole crowd of people up to a half mile away, images felt like starting all over again.

And this vampire attack. That too, felt like we were starting all over again. Because that's what it was, wasn't it? Even if Addison would just end up another abnormal, she had been attacked. Something she hadn't asked for.

In a town where we were supposed to be safe from exactly that.

Chapter 5

Better Than Water

We stood in the alley between the general store and the grocer. There was only one window to choose from, same as the one in my bedroom, but a bit wider and set lower on the wall, which made it easier to climb into.

Ethan, whose fingers had been drumming against the little wooden box since we'd picked it up from his house, opened the window and pushed it up until both panes disappeared into the frame. He stepped over, then held it for Stella. Riah went next and Christian looked at me. *You coming?*

I brushed past him, straightened up once I was inside, and studied the store. Christian slid the panes back into place and left me to wander down an aisle.

It smelled dusty. Musky? I took a few steps to the right and scanned the shelves. The siren facemask Stella told me about last year sat nearby.

Does this stuff really work? I asked her. She was in the next aisle. There were only two.

"What stuff?" She stretched up to peek over the short-er-than-average shelving unit.

"All of it, the Silk in a Bottle shampoo, the Whiter than White toothpaste..."

"No. It probably expires tomorrow. Are you going to use all that by tomorrow?" She dropped back down as I turned the shampoo around. Sure enough, the date on it was only a week away.

I trailed my hand along the shelf, past the makeup and glitter powder, and read the labels of the cleaning supplies across the aisle. They were full of promises to make your house sparkle and keep the dust away for good. A ways down, perfumes and colognes promised devotion, repulsion, or the ability to attract wolves.

Hey, Riah.

"Hey, what?" His head appeared at the end of the aisle.

You'd be fooled by perfume?

"I'm particularly fond of *Contentment*, but I think *Joy* is the best seller."

"That's how they do it? They try to match the smell of an emotion?"

"You just have to figure out which your wolf prefers. It's not worth it, if you ask me. But then, I'd go for a good NEA any day."

"Non-emotive aroma," I sounded out the acronym and picked up a little jar of *Nose Salve.*

"You rub that above your lip if you want to block any incoming odors." He itched hard at the back of his hand, then tossed a hat from the display at the end of the aisle onto my head.

Soft and warm, I reached up to touch it. As soon as my fingers sunk into it though, I snatched it off. "What *is* this?"

"Wolf fur. Very thick, very warm, and very cozy." He smirked, and I sprayed the perfume I was holding at him.

He sniffed. "Ooh, desire. Good thing there's no wolves here or I'd have to peel them off of me."

I squirt him one more time. Catching a scarf around me, he tugged me closer to try to get the bottle out of my hands.

We were laughing, and he was being gentle, but I yelled, "Bananas!" anyway. It was our safe word. He'd bruised my wrist last year while trying to keep me from provoking a wild vampire. After that, he insisted we have a word in case he forgot his own strength again.

'Bananas' was both somewhat difficult and really funny to get out while laughing. Anyway, he stopped and let go of me immediately.

"Did I hurt you?"

"No."

"That's cheating!" he cried.

I laughed and squirt him again. He batted the mist with his hand. "It's just that I have a very important question," I said.

Dumping the scarf back on the end table, he muttered, "What? Cheater."

"How do they get wolf fur off a raging wolf to make these?"

"It's probably dog hair or from the canis lupus."

"False advertising!" I cried, indignant.

"Cheater!" he cried back, with a grin.

The sound of rocks tumbling against each other came from where Christian was standing in the corner. His fingers were rifling through a basket of crystals, and he looked away as soon as I noticed him watching us.

"What are those?" Once closer, I could read the sign: quartz, labradorite, moonstone, and amethyst.

"They're just rocks, but they want you to think they help a dendrite see."

"Like I'd stop getting headaches every time we start something new?" I fingered a smaller one hanging on a cord.

"No, like, see the future."

I shot a look at him. "Like your dreams?"

He shrugged. *I was thinking it might help clarify the one I keep having.* "If you'd have asked me a month ago, I'd have said they were useless."

But he had one picked out. It sat in his palm, cord dangling out of his hand.

I kissed him quick, because I didn't like public displays of affection the way he did, then moved on to study the finger pads hanging nearby. They professed to help draw telelectrical output from the brain and encouraged me to zap my friends and zing my lovers.

I could figure that for a bust on my own.

Riah was browsing the bookshelf wall while scratching the back of his neck, but I headed back up toward the counter to Stella. She was getting a bruise-colored smoothie out of what looked like a Slushie machine.

I noted the bottles of giggle juice across the aisle from where she stood. Giggle juice and Blood-Aid. "What's Blood-Aid?"

"It's like Kool-Aid, but blood. You know, if you're camping or something and don't have a fridge or live person to keep it fresh." She grinned at the face I made. "And this is a vampire smoothie."

I raised my eyebrows.

"It's made from vampire blood and is supposed to be crazy healthy, like a supercharged vitamin. Wanna try?" She slurped a big gulp from the straw.

"No thanks." I pictured the gelatinous ooze I'd seen coming from Ethan's bullet wound last year and was pretty sure I never wanted to ingest it.

"Better than water," she sang to entice me.

I snorted.

We walked up to the counter where Ethan was rifling through the lost and found. The display on this end of the aisle was of Vampire Burnscreen—'to screen out the burn'—and a small fishbowl of fangs.

"Are these real vampire fangs?" I was mildly appalled. "What would someone want with those?"

"A keepsake. You can string them on a necklace and keep your vampire close to your heart." Stella sighed wistfully. "Maybe I should do that."

I gave her a look, and she burst out laughing. "I'm kidding, Grace. I wouldn't do that. Besides, I have a pair at my beck and call." She pried open Ethan's mouth, and he flashed them for her absently, still intent on the lost and found.

"They're sort of a souvenir," Christian explained, as Riah joined us. "Like when normals go to the beach and bring home shells or rocks or shark's teeth."

"But no one is going home from here," I pointed out.

"Right. That's why they're so dusty." He glanced up at the cashier, as if the guy was going to be offended, but he just shrugged.

"Five keys." Ethan's voice had taken a defeated turn, and he was staring at five keys he'd laid out in a row. "Four too big, and one too small." Sliding them off the counter and into his hand, he dumped them back in the lost and found and shoved the box back toward the cashier. "Thanks."

"Good. It's stuffy in here." Riah scratched both his arms at once, like he was trapped beneath his skin. "Let's go."

Stella and Ethan followed him out, slipping through the window for the alley. I looked to Christian, who was still leaning against the counter. *The Complete Dictionary of Tear Formulas* was on the wall behind him. *Why do they bother teaching tear formulas at school?*

He glanced at it. *Each formula in there is missing an ingredient. It's a way to keep the secret. The most important ingredient has to be passed down, word of mouth.* He nodded at the cashier and pointed to it. The cashier checked his eyes, I guess to make sure they sparkled, then handed it to him. Christian offered it to me and pulled out his wallet.

I pushed off my toes and kissed him quick. *I'll pay you back.*

You never have to pay me back, Grace. For anything. That's not what I'm in it for.

"Not in what for?"

He motioned between the two of us. "This."

I slipped around him, since it seemed like a strange place to have this kind of serious conversation, with my friends waiting outside and the cashier watching closely.

I mean it. He caught my arm before I could sneak through the window, which Riah was holding up for me.

I looked from Christian to the window and back. Like, let's go already, they're waiting, and his face fell.

I want you to understand I'd do anything for you. Do anything, be anything, whatever you want.

Holding my new dictionary against my chest, I studied him. "That's really sweet, Christian, but I just want you to be you. That's who I liked in the first place."

He smiled and wrapped his arms around me. "Say that again."

I couldn't help it, I glanced over my shoulder. Riah caught my eye and dropped the window pane. Resting my forehead down against Christian's shoulder, I sighed. "I just want you to be you, Christian Riley. That's who I fell for that very first day." I smirked at this, because we both remembered that first day, and all the hints he'd given me, before Sofia had shown up at his side.

He shook his head. "So much time, wasted." Setting his lips on mine like a whisper, he waited for me to kiss him back. Christian was not the type to need reassurance like this. Part of what I liked about him was that he was so sure of himself. Somehow, though, being with me seemed to make him more insecure.

Is this about your dream? I wondered. Or was it about Riah? Did he say and ask these kinds of things every time he saw me having fun with Riah?

He removed his lips from mine. "Why does it have to be about anything? Why can't it just be about us?"

Right. Well, I didn't feel like starting a fight, so I took the crystal from his hand and draped it around his neck. It hung low. With one more kiss and a smile, I turned and slipped back out the window.

Chapter 6

Sounds Great

Christian was late picking me up for school the next morning.

"You okay?" I asked, as I slid into the car. He was never late.

"I had a rough morning."

I laced my fingers through his and squeezed them, waiting for more, but he was focused on the road. "What happened?" I finally asked.

"I woke up from a very bad dream."

"A dream-dream?"

"It was the same one, but this time Riah took you. Same as before, to the moon so I couldn't get to you. I could sense you, though, was sure you could hear me in your head, but you wouldn't respond." He refused to look in my direction, like he was mad at me about it. About something I did in a dream.

"Christian, I would never hear you and not respond."

"No comment on the Riah part? No 'Oh silly, I'd never leave you for Riah.'" It was the first time he impersonated my voice. I didn't like it.

"So this is about Riah?" Which meant it had probably been about him yesterday too. I considered taking my hand back, but before I could, he clutched on to me the way I'd been clutching on to him.

"I'm waiting."

"Waiting for what?"

He glared at me.

"Are you joking? You honestly need me to tell you I'd never leave you for Riah?"

He parked the car. "Aren't you going to ask me what I think it means?"

"I can tell you what it doesn't mean." I shook off his hand and tried to hold on to my patience. "It doesn't mean Riah is going to bite me and steal me away from you. Only I can steal myself away from you. Only I decide who I'll be with. And if you can't trust that, there isn't anything more I can do about it."

"I think it means he's going to bite you and make you his. Then I'm gone. I'm not important anymore."

And there it went, my patience. "He's not going to bite me. You're being ridiculous." I got out and slammed my door.

"Something about it is always true."

He was right about that, but this dream couldn't be fate or destiny or whatever you wanted to call it. It had to be a warning of some kind or maybe just jealousy rearing its ugly head, which is what I told him.

He didn't like it. And we had entered a busy hallway.

The look on his face was so tortured, I couldn't help coming back partway. *I'm not saying I think it's baloney. I think your dreams are special, and I will be careful to stay away from wolf teeth. But I also think you have to be careful not to let these dreams run your life. You can't stop thinking for yourself because of them.* I stumbled a little as the truth of this hit me. Maybe it was this dream that had stolen some of his confidence. Not me, and not Riah.

I am thinking for myself. No one else's brain is doing the thinking—or the dreaming.

I felt for him, for the anxiety that dream must be breeding, especially since they usually came and went within a week, where this one was recurring and thus indefinite. My irritation faded a little as we reached my locker, but the halls were clearing out. We were going to be late for class. I dumped my jacket and backpack, then tried to step around him, but he stood in my way.

"I want to move into your locker."

"Okay." I took a step.

"Okay?" He blocked me with a pout. "I kind of thought this would be a more exciting moment for us."

We were late for class and had just been arguing. Maybe if he wanted it to be an exciting moment, he should have picked a better time. "Sounds great." Shoving past him, I broke into a run.

Mrs. Smith eyed me as I took my seat and mumbled a quiet apology. Sofia and Emily snickered behind their long, talon-like fingers, and I glared at them with everything I had in me.

The lecture on how vampires came into being was fast and furious. I could barely keep up, but at least it kept me preoccupied.

"Dr. Vampehr, who'd been traveling to study jungle insects, discovered a spider that preyed off mammals. It was very fast, and he was fascinated with how it would climb onto its prey unnoticed, sinking its appendages into the neck for blood. As it was nearly the size of a fist, it could take in much more than your average mosquito, and he noted that smaller mammals didn't survive the bite.

"When he arrived home, his wife found one in his suitcase. He hadn't meant to bring it back, but being that it was there, he collected it in a jar. His wife insisted it bit her, and while he studied her wound, the spider blistered where he'd set it in the sunlight. He'd assumed it indestructible, but it was, after all, just a spider used to the cover of the jungle.

"His wife went into a feverish fit for a week. When she finally came out of it she was feral and uncontrollable, spending the days in bed and the nights hunting. When the authorities came for her, he stood aside. She managed to get away, and he never saw her again. She did leave a trail of bodies in her wake, however, so Vampehr spent the rest of his life trying to rid the jungles of the spiders. They say for every spider he brought into the sunlight, his wife created two vampires.

"We'll talk about Don Augustine Calumet tomorrow, the respected theologian who was the first to claim vampires existed. And we'll discuss exactly how he came to know about them." Mrs. Smith slapped her book shut and asked if any of us had started reading the novel she'd assigned. It was titled *Vampehr to Vampire: Death to Life* and romanticized the factual account of that very first vampire, Dorothy Vampehr.

Dorothy drifted through my thoughts the rest of the morning, until lunch when Riah asked Ethan if he'd heard anything from his cop uncle about Addy's case.

Addy? I asked him. Since when were they on a nickname basis?

He turned toward me, hat backwards. The only way our teachers were okay with hats. "Yes, Addy."

"She didn't see the vampire who bit her," Ethan said. "All she remembers is a stocky not-vampire in front of her. Too dark to make out his face, though."

"A wolf," Christian muttered, his hand absently reaching for the crystal hidden under his shirt.

But it was a vampire bite, I reminded. Not like his dream.

"Maybe the wolf was there to pull the vampire off before it got dangerous," Riah said.

I squinted a little at him. "All attacks are dangerous."

"You think it was planned?" Stella asked.

"It wouldn't have had to be," Ethan said. "If I was the type who wanted to drink fresh, I could see caving if Riah was with me more quickly than if I was alone."

I kept my mouth shut as they kept talking about it like it was a normal conversation to have. None of them were in Addison's position. None of them were at risk. That, or I had no idea what kind of violence existed for most abnormals outside of this town, the ones who lived in the wild and in the shadows. If they did, and the best they could ask for, or expect, was that Addison was still alive in some way, shape, or form...

With a shiver, I crumpled my lunch bag. Christian wrapped an arm around me and asked me if I would walk the halls with him. I leaned my body into his as we went, trying to forget our fight this morning. I couldn't handle vampire bites and fighting all in the same day.

"Where are you taking me?" I asked.

"To move in." With a grin, he opened his locker and piled my arms with books.

"I doubt anyone's going to get attacked at school."

His smile faded. "That's not why I want to share a locker with you."

"You really think I'm next?" I asked.

"I have to think that, because if I don't, and you are, and I didn't try to stop it..." Clenching his jaw, he closed his locker.

It was then I realized, that to him, there was no difference between a dream of fate or one of warning. Either way, he felt the responsibility to figure it out and keep me safe from whatever might be coming. And after Addy, I guess I couldn't brush it off as easily as I had that morning.

In that moment, I forgave him for everything.

Then he had to go and say, "I think I put Riah's face on the wolf because I don't like how close you two are."

Wait. Was that why his jaw was set? "He's my best friend." I reminded. I don't know how many times I had to clarify. "You don't see me sharing a locker with him, do you?"

"Your lockers are nearly on top of each other as it is."

"Are you... Wait. Are you moving into my locker so you can keep an eye on us?"

"I'm moving into your locker because I think we're at that point now," he said, a little steelier than I would've liked.

Whatever, I did not want to argue. We made one trip, bringing only the necessities, as the true test was finding room in my messy space.

We were still moving my stuff around when Sofia, Emily, and Aster turned into the hall. "Are they doing what I think they're doing?" Sofia asked as they stopped at her locker. She made sure her voice carried.

"It looks like it," Emily replied, doing the same. The two of them eyed Aster.

"What are you looking at me for?" she clipped. "I don't know what they're doing."

"Aren't you her friend?" The disgust in Sofia's voice was clear. I raised my eyebrows at Christian.

"Yes," Aster shot back. "But they didn't send out a bulletin."

Aster had been taking crap for being my lab partner, for talking to me when we ran into each other at school, and for texting me on occasion. I wondered if Sofia knew that the four of us—Christian, Kevin, Aster, and I—were going to Christian's after school that afternoon. And I wondered what she'd do if Aster and I ever hung out alone together, the two of us.

"It's revolting," Sofia seethed. "Did you hear that down there, Grace? You're revolting!"

I kicked myself for looking over at the sound of my name. I didn't have the energy today to do anything but ignore her. Vampire bites, fighting with Christian, and challenging Sofia? No, thank you.

"Ignore her." Christian took the books from my arms and placed them in the space we'd created. "She's just jealous."

"Jealous of what? She can't be jealous of you anymore, she has a man."

"She can always find something to be jealous about. It's kind of her M.O. She's probably jealous of you and Aster."

I looked over at my new friend and caught her eye. She was frowning at me, or maybe at the whole situation. Sofia stepped in front of her and took a few steps toward me.

"Maybe jealous I never shared a locker with her." Christian closed the door and pulled me to him, effectively wrenching my gaze from the vulture. "Even when I thought I was in love with her, I got my fill."

"You thought you were in love with her?" He thought he was in love with her but never wanted to share her locker? What did that mean about me?

"Right. That's what I said." A slow grin overtook his face and he squeezed me tighter. "I thought I was in love with her, but now I know I wasn't."

I blinked. I guess we had been together for almost a year. I guess I loved him too. Was that okay to say—I guess I love you too? Except he hadn't really said it, and now I was freaking out. Was I supposed to say it or not?

But he seemed happy, just like this, and he pecked me on the nose. "*That's* why I want to share a locker with you."

I reached my arms around him. "I'm sorry I ruined it."

"You couldn't ruin anything if you tried."

I gave him a look because that was baloney. Then Sofia charged into him as she walked past, sending him into me and me into the locker.

"I'm more worried about her than a stupid wolf bite," I admitted. "Wait. What would happen if I got bit by a wolf anyway?"

"If he didn't tear you into pieces, you'd turn into one."

When we pulled up at Christian's house, Aster and Kevin were already there. Kevin was dribbling the ball around the drive, and

Aster was sitting in the yard. The stately stone house stretched out over the water beyond the garage.

Aster and I had the same birthday and the same favorite color. We liked the same music and the same movies. We thought alike and laughed at all the same things. Sometimes I wondered if we were the same person, or twins separated at birth, until I remembered that she was a wolf and I was a dendrite, and we had totally different tastes in guys.

Kevin was fine and all, but I would never go for him. And though we liked the same movies, we did not like the same actors. She liked clean-cut and on the cocky side of arrogant. I liked a little messy and modestly confident. She went for standoffish and cool. I went for approachable and warm. She wanted quiet and reserved. I wanted funny.

I was glad we were hanging out today, because I wanted to talk to her about Addison Jacobs. I knew she wouldn't spare my feelings like Riah or look at the bright side like Stella. She'd also answer any question I threw at her with utter honesty.

As Christian joined Kevin in the driveway, I jumped right into it. "Why does this vampire attack not bother anyone?"

"It's mildly disturbing." She shrugged. "But the police are on it."

"She was attacked. No matter what, that alone should be greatly disturbing."

"Fair point," she agreed. "But werewolves attack things on a regular basis, and every vampire dreams of sinking their teeth into real flesh."

I coughed on some spit, but not really. Really I was coughing on all the vampires around me thinking that on a regular basis. I was coughing on the memory of Ethan at lunch. To find out how good it really tastes, he'd said. Really good. Amazing

"I mean, at night, while they sleep, not like daydreams. Not while they're talking to you."

Taking a deep breath, I reminded myself that this was my home now. "So it wouldn't bother you if you woke up a vampire?"

She shook her head without hesitation. "It'd be a nice break not to change every month."

Okay, so she was obviously coming at this from an altogether different place than I was. Changing form was not new to her, and drinking blood was not a stretch from raw meat. Maybe she couldn't understand.

"But don't you think, of all the abnormals, that a vampire would be the hardest to be?" I ticked the reasons off on my fingers: "They're the most dangerous, the hardest to control, the furthest from human..."

She raised an eyebrow at me. "You haven't seen the power of a crazed wolf."

"But wolves don't like to kill. They're out of their minds. They can't help it."

She pulled her gaze off Kevin's very impressive three-pointer and set it on me. "We like to kill, Grace. You can make excuses for us, but we like to kill. In fact, we probably like it more than the vampires do. They just want the blood."

"But that's the hardest part for Riah, the killing."

"It's probably the *liking* to kill that's the hardest part for him. If I had more of a conscience, it'd be hard for me too."

"You don't... It doesn't bother you?" I stammered. "Not at all?"

She studied her shoes. "No. Does that make me a bad person? If it were a human, I'd be mortified. But the fact that it's an animal? That's what they're there for, you know? Food chain and all that. You eat them too, just cooked and after they don't look gruesome anymore. What's the difference, really?"

"I guess."

She looked over at me, concerned. I recalled that look. Riah had it sometimes, when he was worried what I thought of him.

"You're right. It's totally the food chain." I nodded. "It's just I don't think of you as an animal. I think of you as a human. A human with a monthly blip."

I'd meant it to lighten the mood, but she frowned. "One of my brothers died during one of those monthly blips."

I stared at her. She had one older brother, in my brother Justin's class. He was not dead. "One of your brothers?"

She nodded. "All wolves have litters. You never wondered what happened to the rest of us?"

"The rest of you?" I whispered.

"My older brother Adam was a twin. A twin of a stillborn. It's not uncommon that a dendrite body can't handle the wolf litters. So anyway, I was a quintuplet."

"That's...five." I could barely get it out, because she was the only one left.

"We were born at twenty-four-and-three-quarter weeks. Two of us died in the hospital, then my sister passed when we were two. She had all sorts of problems and eventually...Anyway, I was always the strong one, or so they say. So then it was me and my brother Alex." She paused, her eyes wet. "He died when we were nine and a half. It was a hunting accident. It was stupid, and not my dad's fault, but my mom blamed him. Or maybe she just didn't handle it very well. My dad moved out later that year."

I exhaled heavily. "Do you still see him? Your dad?"

"He has us for the full moon. Because of my mom being a dendrite."

"That's it, once a month?"

"He's kind of a hermit. My mom buys him groceries and supplies that we take when we go. I mean, you might think Shady Woods is the middle of nowhere, but you haven't seen nowhere until you've been to his house." There was a pause. Then she continued, as an afterthought, "We could probably stay at his house for the full moon instead of traveling. I'm pretty sure it'd be safe, but I think he likes to get out once in awhile."

"I'm so sorry, Aster." The closest I came to someone I loved dying was leaving Charlie and my other friends behind in Chicago.

"It's life, Grace, no big deal. Sucks sometimes, and then other times,"—her eyes fell on Kevin, who was bent over, catching his breath—"it surprises you."

Christian walked over and fell on the grass next to me. Kevin headed down to the water.

"Where's he going?" I asked.

"For a swim."

"Now?"

Christian eyed me. It was a look I hadn't gotten in a long time, since last year when I knew almost nothing about life here.

"Right." I nodded. "Siren."

Aster hopped up to follow Kevin as a car turned into the driveway. Dr. Riley. I bit my lip. "Will you ask him about Addison?"

"Of course."

I helped him up, and we followed his dad's car into the garage.

"So, Dad," Christian tapped his fingertips on the top of his father's sedan as he got out. "Any news on Addison?"

He had Christian's exact hair, only it was brown instead of black. Christian had gotten the black hair from his mother. "She's good. On a continuous blood drip to keep her happy."

"How long will she be in the hospital?" I asked.

"Another month or so, until she's through the worst of it. Then we'll take her off the IV. After that, her parents will keep her home for a few more weeks so she can have access to blood whenever she wants it. Then she should be good and under control." He patted Christian on the shoulder before taking the little ramp from the garage over the water and into the house.

"How much blood does a vampire have to drink to kill a person?"

Christian wrapped his arms around my waist and waddled me back to our spot on the grass. "As much blood as you'd have to lose before you die."

"And if you don't drink enough blood to kill them, that's how they become a vampire? Anywhere from one bite to not dying?" I was glad he'd wrapped himself around me. It was a nice distraction from the conversation.

"Right, but most wilds drain every body they come across, since they don't know when their next meal will be."

I curled against him, my face to his neck, which was slightly clammy from basketball. "So you can't drink from a human without killing or turning them?"

"If they drink from a cut, no bite—no vampire saliva reaching the deeper tissues—you'd be fine. As long as they didn't drink enough to kill you."

I responded to that with a full-body shiver, even though the sun was warm and my sweater cozy. Christian placed his hands on either side of my face and kissed me. I tried to focus on that, tried to pretend we were normal. Tried to pretend that this was all normal.

Maybe it really was now.

Chapter 7

I Can Smell You Like a Book

Riah's birthday had crept up on me, and suddenly I was a complete failure of a best friend.

"Frustrated?" he asked, as we met up in the hall for Spanish.

"I'm trying to come up with something awesome for your birthday," I admitted, putting up a hand. "I know, I should have planned ahead."

He shrugged. "I did."

"You did what?"

"Planned ahead."

"You made plans without me?"

"It's not like that."

I was silent the rest of the way to class, but by the time we took our seats I could no longer contain myself. "Who do you have plans with?"

"Myself."

"What?"

"I'm going for a walk in the woods."

"By yourself?"

"By myself."

Well, that I could handle without a hurt ego. "Why by yourself?"

"I don't want company."

"Oh." Ego, hurt.

He shifted towards me slightly and took an imperceptible breath in. "Why are you disappointed?"

"I'm not disappointed."

"Grace, I can smell you like a book. Don't you get that by now?"

"You don't smell a book, Riah. The expression is—"

"Yes, I know what the expression is. I changed it. You know what I mean. Save us the time and tell me why you're disappointed."

I sighed. "I wanted to make it special." To be quite honest, it sounded like the perfect way for Riah to celebrate his birthday.

"Then come."

"You just said you wanted to be alone."

"You're as good as being alone."

I wrinkled my nose. This conversation was only getting worse.

He laughed. "Let me rephrase that. Your company would be the only company I'd prefer to my own. Stella and Ethan just make out in front of me, and I didn't want a big thing with them and you and Christian and my sisters and their friends. I just want to chill. Anyway, you get the picture."

"I get the picture."

"The picture you get does not include Christian, right?"

I gave him an I'm-not-an-idiot look.

"I'm not going to be the third wheel on my birthday," he continued. "If your boyfriend has a problem with it, I'll go back to my original plan."

"He won't have a problem with it." Well, he probably would. But it wasn't his call.

<hr>

At lunch, Aster let the cat out of the bag when she stopped by our table to see if I wanted to come over after school.

"I can't. It's Riah's birthday."

"Ugh." She rolled her eyes melodramatically. "I tell you, that Riah..."

Riah kissed in her direction, and she palmed his face. He bit at her in response, but she pulled away just in time and with a little wave was on her way.

"I didn't know it was your birthday," Christian said. "Happy Birthday."

"Yeah, thanks."

Christian leaned in toward me. "So, party after school?"

"He wants to go on a walk in the woods," Ethan said, draping an arm across the back of Stella's chair. "By himself. No party."

Riah, very nonchalantly, said, "Grace is coming."

Christian's gaze flickered between us. "Just Grace?"

I was going to tell you in gym.

Just the two of you?

Right.

That's not okay.

I hope you aren't implying that you have any say in whether it's okay or not.

I'm not implying anything but my extreme displeasure.

Well, imply it to someone else.

Just the two of you is a date.

It's not a date. You have to like someone for it to be a date.

You like him.

You know what I mean.

I was saved by the bell. Holy glad for that right now. Pushing away from the table, I stormed off.

We met back up in gym, but gym wasn't the best time to talk, so we seethed through a game of soccer and into skills, where we sat down quietly and pretended to listen to Mr. Turner's short lecture. As soon as we were let loose, it started.

How would you feel if I went off with Addison for an afternoon?

I wouldn't care. I paused. *Wait. Why Addison?*

Because she's single, and she's cute.

I squirmed in my seat. I didn't like that.

All I'm saying is Riah's not a chump.

Mr. Turner was eyeballing us, as if he could tell we weren't sending pictures. I held my head in my hands to make it look like I was working, like the effort hurt. *It doesn't matter. What matters is you're being silly. I wouldn't keep you from your friends. Girl or boy.*

Christian repositioned himself in his seat, the fight in him subsiding a little. *What about Addison?*

Dragging my hands from my head down over my face, I stared at him. *Seriously what about her? Are you telling me that if I do this today on my best friend's birthday, you're going to ask Addison to spend the afternoon with you?*

With that, he softened the rest of the way, his foot sliding across the aisle to meet mine. *No, I'm sorry, that was stupid. I mean, what about her bite? You should not be willingly walking into the woods right now.*

I'll be with Riah.

Christian's jaw hardened. *Riah is not indestructible.*

He can smell danger from a mile away.

Vampires are faster than that.

Addison was alone. By herself. But it was making me fidget. He was right. I didn't want to put myself in the way of that. It was

Riah's birthday, though, and I needed to make that special. I'd been a crappy friend since Christian and I started dating, and what Riah said about Ethan and Stella making out in front of him... he must feel like the third wheel all the time. I wouldn't let it happen on his birthday, and I wouldn't let him be alone, either.

I'm just worried about you, Grace. I can't help it.

We stared at each other for a moment. He took his foot back from mine and folded over his desk, resting his head on his arms.

And fine. Maybe a little part of me wants to be your best friend too. Is it so ridiculous that I want to be everything to you?

You can't be everything to me, I said, delivering it as gently as I could. *No one person can be everything.*

You really believe that?

You really don't?

The bell rang. We were both silent as we gathered our things, filed out of class, and walked to our locker.

Riah was waiting at his, which did feel slightly on top of mine at the moment. I went first, packing my bag before turning back to face my boyfriend. He kissed my nose, my cheek, my lips, while Riah studied the opposite end of the hall.

"I hope that's all you can think of," Christian muttered when I pulled away. "The whole time you're with Riah."

I sighed, one hand on his chest. "I'll call you when I get home."

"Then maybe we can talk about what I can't be for you that he can."

Biting back a frown, I unwrapped his arms from around me. For starters, Riah did not put any pressure on me. No expectations.

He definitely didn't expect to be all I needed. If that wasn't a lot of pressure, I didn't know what was.

Riah's after-school snack consisted of six eggs, two bananas, and a raw steak.

Once that was taken care of, we headed out his back door, across his small lawn, and into the forest. Before long, I could have spun in a circle and not known which way was up. With a deep breath, I took in the sweet smell of fall: cool and muddy, crisp and decomposed. It was enough to soothe me.

"Christian's worried about us being out here, after what happened to Addy."

"It's so nice of him to be worried about me."

I shoved into him, and his smirk. "You're not, though?"

He glanced over at me, quickly. "You are?"

This was too much like my previous conversation. "I trust you, and your sense of smell."

"I'd never let anything happen to you."

"I know."

"But Christian doesn't."

"Oh, I think he does." That was part of the problem. He couldn't understand how Riah would be willing to protect me without wanting anything in return.

Riah moved a fallen tree off the path in front of us. A real, normal-sized tree.

"We could have just stepped over that."

"It was a trip hazard." He stopped in front of a newer branch that hung face level over the path, snapping it in two and tossing it into the brush. Then back to the topic at hand. "What's up with you two lately?"

"What do you mean?"

"Your relationship smells a little off. I thought it was just that he was jealous, but if he trusts me, then what is it?"

"Um, hold please. Did you just say you can smell our relationship?"

He nodded and I stopped, needing time for my brain to wrap itself around this one.

"That's what we're working on in skills, how to read where emotions intersect when two people are together. What it means."

"And we smell off?"

He started walking again. "Most relationships have an edge at some time or another. Lots of them have it all the time."

"So when we're fighting…"

"Not worth trying to hide it." He tapped his nose.

Christian wouldn't want me spilling his dreams and jealousies to anyone, let alone Riah, but Riah had sniffed it out.

He poked me and I looked over at him. "I'm still your best friend." It was a statement, not a question. "I won't tell a soul. Think of it as furthering my education."

At this point it was tell him or lie, which he'd also be able to smell. Whatever. I probably trusted him more than I trusted anyone, normal or abnormal. "He can be too much. He wants too much."

"You mean, like... he pressures you?" Riah glanced down the length of me, but was clearly uncomfortable about it.

"No, no. Not like that. He's a perfect gentleman."

"He better be."

I sighed at how that, at least, would be less complicated and easier to walk away from. "It's the rest of me he wants, I guess."

He raised an eyebrow but didn't immediately reply. Our footsteps fell, the wind blew the scent of pines into and through me, and a chipmunk crossed our path.

Riah broke the silence. "What exactly does that mean?"

"I don't know. We haven't finished arguing about it yet."

"Is this about the locker?" He elbowed me, grinning to lighten the mood. "Were you not ready to move in together?"

I shoved at him, but my strength had no effect. He was a block of stone. It would have been much more satisfying if he'd stumbled off the path. "There's a dream that has him all worked up, so I'm trying to be patient about it. Maybe it's that he's desperate to keep me safe, rather than desperate to be all I need, you know?"

"One of his dream-dreams?"

"Do you think that if he has a dream, if he knows what to look for, that he could change the outcome?" I glanced over at Riah. "He's always believed it was out of his hands, but now he's trying to control how it plays out."

"What's so different about this particular dream that he wants to control the outcome?"

I took a deep breath, preparing to explain it as delicately as I could. "A certain wolf bites me and takes me to the moon," Okay, that wasn't delicate. It's like I wanted to tell him. But of course I did. He was my best friend. I shook my head and tried again. "Christian searches for me, can sense that I'm close, but when he calls to me, I don't want to be found. I'm trapped by this wolf, but he doesn't think it bothers me like it should. He thinks I'm literally going to be bitten by a wolf, and he's going to lose me forever."

"Wow. Dude's got some abandonment issues, huh?"

"Riah," I warned.

"Sorry. Who's the certain wolf?"

I raised my brow.

He burst out with his big laugh. "Me?"

I nodded and waited for him to stop laughing.

It dwindled to a chuckle before petering out to a frown. "He actually thinks I'm going to bite you?"

"No, he thinks he put your face on the wolf because..." I hung my head. How did he get me to do that? Get me to tell him everything just like that. Was it enough of an excuse that he could smell it?

He clicked his tongue. "So many secrets you're keeping these days."

"But that's the problem!" I groaned. "I'm not keeping them."

"Don't worry, I'll keep them. He'll never know."

I sighed. "He's jealous of you, of us."

"Ah, so I was right." His brow furrowed. "But this was a wolf in his dream, not a vampire?"

"Yes. And he had the first dream before school even started, before Addison even got bit. Maybe it's just a warning to be careful. Maybe he could sense that was coming, and now it's happened. Now it's over."

"But the dream didn't stop." He exhaled hard. "Of course he's trying to change the outcome. I would too."

"Let's be realistic, though. His dreams usually play out literally, but this one can't. I'm not going to end up on the moon. I kind of thought it was more about intuition, like he picks up subconsciously on a bunch of clues the rest of us are missing. I can buy that, and that makes sense when they play out within the week. But I'm not sure I can buy this far-out-in-the-future fortune teller thing."

Riah shrugged. "When I'm a wolf, all I go on is instinct. Put Christian's ancient siren knowledge together with the brain power of a dendrite and maybe he is a fortune teller. Who knows?"

"He isn't the only siren dendrite around here. You're telling me they all have dreams?"

"No, but I think you're being too particular about it." He went to snap another hanging branch to get it out of the way for me, but then stopped and sniffed its lone, curling leaf. Letting go, he took a few steps, sniffing the air around us in a circle. "Speaking of, it smells like a werewolf has been here."

"Yeah." I smirked. "You."

"No. A wolf in wolf form. Like, on the full moon." He took a few more steps, pulling more branches to him as he went.

"No one hunts in these woods, Riah. I'm sure it's nothing."

Dropping to his knees, he brought the underbrush to his nose. "What if the wilds are back?" he muttered. "What if that's who got Addy?"

"You're calling her Addy again?"

Sitting back on his heels, he looked up at me. "Grace, she lives down the street from me. We grew up playing Kick the Can."

I shook my head of it. "Okay, so my boyfriend's been dreaming of a wolf bite, Addison saw one when she was attacked, and now you're telling me there's proof someone was hunting here last weekend?"

"Unless you're doubting my sense of smell, that's exactly what I'm telling you."

Chapter 8

Sofia Is (Maybe Not) Always a Bad Idea

Riah's discovery was confirmed by his dad and a few others, so we were all on alert the next few weeks. But when nothing else happened, no wild camp found, it was assumed a wolf had simply passed through. An accident. A one-off. They also decided it couldn't be related to Addy, because a wolf on the full moon wouldn't be traveling with a vampire.

Besides, no one in Shady was going to miss the carnival. Not even me. Not this year.

I was in full-body leather, à la the vampire show that was the current rage. The fact that there were seven main characters was the only reason Sofia agreed to let me be a part of it. To show

Christian I wasn't trying to completely disrupt his friend group, I agreed.

My mom dropped me at Christian's because his house was closest to the beach. We planned to walk from there. Apparently parking was a pain, and Sofia insisted on us making an entrance.

Christian grinned when he opened the wide front door, grabbed my hand, and led me through the spacious rooms to the back deck and its sleek, multi-level walkway that ended on a platform surrounded by lily pads.

There, he fished a small box out of his pocket. "It's one year tomorrow since our first kiss."

I suppose technically that would be our one year anniversary. Crap. I was as bad with anniversaries as I was with birthdays.

Snapping the box open, he held it out for me to inspect. Two chains with one hammered gold disc on each, his first initial on the bottom edge of one, mine on the bottom edge of the other.

"Oh," I muttered, with a hand to my chest.

"You like it." He let out a heavy breath and smiled. Only with him relaxing into himself did I realize how nervous he'd been.

I nodded, returning his grin, and hurried to put it on. The chain with the 'g' hung low, while the one with the 'c' settled between my collarbones.

"I didn't know if it was too much."

"The perfect amount of much," I assured, meaning it. We still hadn't come to an agreement about where the boyfriend stopped and the friend began, or why he couldn't be both. And after a few days of arguing about it every chance he got, we'd both started avoiding the discussion.

Wrapping my hand around the lower chain, I thanked him with kisses. Lots of them, quick and haphazard, until we were both laughing into it.

The back door slid open. Aster emerged from behind Kevin, and I squealed. She was in ripped-up 80's attire, a weapon belt slung loosely around her waist, and her long hair interspersed with tiny braids like her character on the show.

"You look perfect!" I cried as she hugged me.

Kevin was in a three-piece suit, and Christian looked pretty much like me because our characters were siblings. Sofia's idea, of course.

"Everyone's here," Kevin said, holding the door open.

We filed in, following him through the house to where Jeremy was leaning against Emily's car and laughing with Sofia about something. She stopped laughing as soon as she saw me, immediately scanning us with narrowed eyes, probably making sure our costumes were up to her specifications.

As we reached them, she snapped her fingers. "What the hell is that?"

I glanced down to where she was studying my chest. The necklace.

"Part of the costume, actually." Christian winked at me. I grinned, because he was right. The girl I was playing had necklaces just like these for her and her brother. They'd been a final gift from her mom to remind them to stick together. He leaned in. "Wish I could say I was just that good, but it is where I got the idea."

Sofia stepped forward and I stepped back, but she was too quick for me. Her fist closed around the top coin. I winced, waiting for the yank that would break the chain and release it from my neck. But then Aster's hand was there, on top of hers.

Sofia seethed, "You're crushing my fingers."

"Then let go," Aster said. "You wouldn't want to ruin the costumes you so diligently planned."

Sofia dropped it but stepped into me. I went to shove her back but Jeremy yanked her away before I had the chance. Christian slid a hand between us too, stopping me from advancing on her.

We stared each other down anyway, held back by Christian and Jeremy, though I wasn't sure from what exactly. I had no intention of fighting her, had just wanted her out of my space.

"I should've planned for you to be a victim." Flipping her fangs down, she flashed them. "Better typecasting."

"I'll show you to the herd of dendrites when we get to the festival," Emily added, always trying to get the last word.

I swallowed hard. The connotation of the word "herd" was not lost on me.

"What the hell's gotten into you?" Aster hissed.

Sofia and Emily ignored the question. Instead, they stalked off, Emily a beat behind Sofia.

"The necklace has gotten into her," I muttered. "Her new boyfriend won't even dress up with her, and her old boyfriend's making it romantic. Of course she's mad."

"Her new boyfriend is what's gotten into her," Jeremy said. "Micah is kind of a dick, and totally a purist."

Sofia glanced over her shoulder. "Are you guys coming or what?"

Jeremy went first, then Kevin, then Aster, the three of them walking together on the road behind Sofia and Emily. Christian took my hand. "This was a bad idea."

"Sofia is always a bad idea."

"She wasn't always like this."

Flashing a soft smile at him, I said, "That's what all ex-boyfriends say."

"No, I'm talking way back. Elementary school."

It was the first time he'd offered up any information on why he'd ever been into her. I took the opening. "How'd you two end up together?"

Christian rubbed at his forehead. "She can be gentle, if you're gentle with her first. And you don't always see people as mean, if you knew them before they were mean."

"When did you start seeing it?" Because he did now, and regularly.

"When she got mean about you." He wrapped an arm around me, and I rubbed my hands together. November first was cold. I was thankful for the full-body leather. "I should have broken up with her then, but we'd been together so long. She always knew when to lay on the gentle. And, to be honest, you're kind of intimidating."

I laughed and sunk against him as we walked, the deserted street starting to grow busier. More cars slid past, looking for a spot, and more noise carried from the park. "No way I'm scarier than she is."

He kissed my forehead. "But you were, because what you thought of me mattered more than what she did."

I smiled.

"For the record, she's not mean for no reason."

I eyed him, but he had his attention set on the edge of the crowd ahead of us. When he didn't offer more, I prodded him. "What does that mean?"

"Vampires heal nearly instantaneously, which means they make for pretty easy punching bags."

I blinked, studying him harder.

"None of us were surprised when she got mean because of what she dealt with at home. Partly our fault, probably. We gave her a lot of leeway for it in the beginning. Maybe still do."

The musicians began to test their mics. I looked away from him as we entered the crowd. It was buzzing with smiles and excited chatter, the energy contagious.

"Does that change how you feel about me?" Christian asked. We wove between the scattered bonfires and the people curled around them.

"What do you mean?"

"I've been worried what you thought of me for dating her, when she's been so awful to you."

I stopped, which meant he stopped with me. The crowd's current changed to flow around us, like we were an island in a river. He had an amazing habit of choosing the worst times for these kinds of conversations. Always, it seemed, in public. Maybe he felt there was less pressure that way, an easier out if it got too uncomfortable for me.

What did I think of him for dating her? "I can't say it doesn't make some sense when you put it that way."

I'm serious, Grace. I've been nervous trying to think how I'd explain it to you.

It makes you human, Christian. And sensitive. It shows how willing you are to hold up other people when they need it. Even if you get nothing in return. How can I not like that about you?

You're sure?

The only thing I'm not real comfortable with is how it makes me very sad for her. Vampires were easy punching bags, he was right. No trace for your teacher to snort out, or your best friend's parents. Your word against an adult's.

He wrapped his arms tightly around me and whispered, soft and sweet, directly into my head, *I cannot get enough of you.*

Placing fingertips on either side of his face, I drew him down to kiss me. This had become my go-to when he pulled out the fancy words for me. His mouth and cheeks were warm, but I knew my hands were cold. He'd flinched when they landed on his cheeks.

"Bonfire," I said. We needed a bonfire.

"Lots of them, come on." Taking my hand, he led me further into the mass of people, squished together because everyone needed a spot inside the park.

People roasted marshmallows and chunks of meat. I even caught sight of an Oreo on a stick. I guess the rule was whatever you could skewer. As the band got started, a huge bucket of hard candies rained down on us. I ducked into Christian as he pointed Stella out. She was marking Riah's sisters with siren tears so their faces would glow in the dark. When she caught sight of us, she beamed, sliding over to me with the last bit on her finger. Down my cheek, along my neck... There, her finger stopped and she let out a squeal.

"What?" Riah glanced over from where he was talking to Addison.

I gaped at her, now taller than Riah, as Stella poked at me and squealed again.

Riah squinted in the low light. "Is that a promise necklace or something?"

"It's just a necklace." I stuck my tongue out at him. He tried to grab it.

I went to kick him in the shin, but he caught my leg with his. I punched him in the stomach. That only hurt me, though, considering how tight his superhuman werewolf muscles were. Grabbing my wrist, he twisted it behind my back.

I would never win.

Riah smelled my submission and let me go with an evil grin, but that left us standing awkwardly in front of Christian's not-so-happy face, as if we'd just remembered he was there.

"Why can't it be a promise necklace?" Christian asked.

Riah raised an eyebrow at me and did a dramatic turn back to Addison.

"It can be." I fiddled with it. It could be, but we were sophomores in high school, and I wasn't even sure yet if I wanted to live abnormal the rest of my life.

Christian stepped forward to kiss the chain where it sat on my neck. Over his shoulder, I had a clear view of Sofia and her boyfriend at the next bonfire. They were fighting, nearly spitting at each other the way their words were coming out of their mouths. When he stormed toward the street, Sofia wiped at her eyes and raced into the woods.

"Why is no one following her?" I asked Christian, pulling my phone out of my pocket to text Aster that Sofia obviously needed someone.

He lifted his head from my neck. "Huh?"

"Sofia and what's-his-name just got in a terrible fight, and she's off crying in the woods. Emily and Aster watched her go."

"They know better," he replied. "You think she's mean normally, you should see her when she's upset."

"Maybe they missed it."

"They didn't miss it."

Well, that was crummy, and I was almost tempted to go after her myself. Was that stupid? "Maybe I should go check on her."

He sort of snorted and sort of laughed, all in one huff. "For *why*?"

My whole outlook of her was skewed now. It had to be why I was feeling so sympathetic. "To make sure she's okay."

He laughed big. Like I was joking.

I pouted. "You go, then. I bet she wouldn't mind if it were you."

"After all she's said to you, comforting her is the last thing I'd do."

"Fine, I'll go." Instead, though, I played a little with the zipper on my shirt.

You're crazy. And asking for it.

I can handle it. I could handle anything. Right?

Right. Of course I could. A person had to. That's what you did. Whatever came up, you handled it. I could handle it.

Then again, they didn't tell you to go walking into it.

With a shrug, I headed for the path, wishing the carnival wasn't so loud. I couldn't hear anything but the noise of it, the music and the crowd, but she was easy to find. Not too far into the tree cover, she sat on a fallen log.

"What do you want?" she grumbled, but with a definite sniffle.

"Are you okay?"

"I'm fine." She rubbed her nose on her sleeve. "My grandma just died, so if you wouldn't mind, I'd like to be alone."

"Your grandma didn't just die."

"She might as well have."

"You probably shouldn't—" Hands clamped onto my shoulders from behind. Sofia shot forward and knocked me to the ground before I could make sense of what was happening. She was tumbling with someone off the path, rolling through the underbrush.

Hopping up from where I fell, I scrambled over to try to pull her off him. She could fight, that was for sure. Definitely knew what she was doing more than Riah had last year when the Hand was after us.

She was on top of someone, struggling with his hood, and I was on top of her. "Sofia, stop!"

Someone else tossed me off her. I landed hard in a soft patch of ferns, but before I could steady myself, she landed like a ragdoll next to me, against a tree. Just like that, we were alone again. Whoever the two of them had been, they disappeared into the shadows in an instant.

I gaped at her. Then at the space the two had gone. "What was that?"

Wiping her face with the back of her hand, she left a bloody smear. A cut above her eyebrow knit itself shut before my eyes. Apparently raccoon blood wasn't necessary for superficial wounds.

"Are you okay?" I asked again.

Her expression, which had been soft when I'd found her and shocked a moment ago, reset itself to its normal glare. "I'm peachy," she snapped, spitting in my direction.

Scooting out of the way, I stood up. "Seriously, what just happened?"

Struggling to stand, she popped a limp shoulder back into its socket with a cry. My eyes about bulged out of my head.

"Shit, Sofia."

"Shut up, Grace."

"What just happened?" I cried. "Who was that?"

"I don't know, but I'm pretty sure you were about to be the next Addison Jacobs." She swept out of the woods. When I realized she'd left me there, I hurried after her.

I should have paid better attention to what they looked like. I should have been scared. Not that I'd had much time to be scared. When I'd felt those hands on my shoulders, I thought it was Emily coming to check on her, or that Aster had gotten my text.

Even after Addison, my mind hadn't gone to any attack. Instead, I'd assumed it was Sofia, starting something because she was angry, vulnerable, and exposed. It hadn't occurred to me that she was protecting me. And it happened so fast that their dark clothing, their lack of costume, hadn't registered either. They weren't there for the festival.

Now I stood surrounded by my people, speechless and in shock, while Riah chewed out Christian for letting me walk into the woods alone. Christian had pulled his crystal from beneath his shirt and was rubbing it frantically, like a genie might pop out.

"Do you not care about her at all?"

"Riah, would you be quiet?" Stella hissed. Because the lecture was doing all sorts of awful things to Christian's face.

I swallowed hard in the realization that Sofia had saved me from becoming herself. Because I would end up an angry, vicious vampire, just like her, if someone forced me into that.

My gaze flitted over to where she sat at the next bonfire. She was watching me, calmly though, not the way she normally did. As soon as I caught her eye, she looked away.

Ethan came back with his uncle, and I spent half an hour trying to see something in my memory that would be of any help. When he headed over to Sofia, she snarled up at him.

"If it's the same guys who got Addison," I said to Riah, "I don't think they were wilds." All I registered, really, was their body shapes. "The vampire wasn't so skinny, not like the ones last year. Which means the wolf you smelled probably wasn't a wild, either, why no one could find any trace of them."

"One of them was a wolf, though?" he asked.

I nodded. "Or a bodybuilder."

"Do you think this was my dream?" Christian asked. "Maybe you're safe now."

"Until the next time you let her do something stupid," Riah snapped.

I put a hand on his arm to shush him, which Christian twitched at. Stella opened her arms in front of me and I stepped forward. She wrapped me up in them, and in her charm. It seeped into me, heavy in a good way, anchoring and soothing.

"Thank you," I whispered.

"Want me to tell them you are perfectly capable of doing stupid things yourself, without them having to 'let' you?"

I laughed. I couldn't help it. And I squeezed her tighter.

Chapter 9

Start Pure In the New Year

As I rushed out the door the next morning, my heel slid on a piece of paper. I reached down for it, noting that it was one of many. Bright red sheets blew along the sidewalk in the brisk wind, stuck out from behind mailbox flags, and had been slipped under windshield wipers.

Christian honked, even though he saw me, and I figured that had something to do with what was in my hand:

START PURE IN THE NEW YEAR

Why do Shady wolves go to so much trouble when it would be easier for the rest of town to stay in one night? Why do Shady vampires have to suffer when they could drink fresh from clean cuts? Pacifism is an illusion, not a compromise. Harmony = Supporting each other's true natures, not just protecting the weak.

I slid into the car, realizing only when I closed the door how much noise came with all those papers rustling in the wind. Christian sneered at the one in my hand. "Tear that up."

"They're not exactly wrong." I took the time to read it again. "Why should the werewolves have to travel so far for one night when we could just lock our doors?"

"This close to civilization?" He gaped at me. "Riah wouldn't even agree with you here."

I looked out the window. "Aster would."

We were starting with third period that day, the morning after the carnival, so it wasn't long before I was able to ask her how she felt about the flyers.

"It's only November," she muttered. "Is this a campaign or something?"

Jeremy leaned forward from his desk on her other side. "Cut your shoulder and I'll spring for dinner, that's what I think about them."

Aster shoved him with her werewolf strength, causing him to slide out of his chair onto the floor. Without missing a beat, he pulled himself back up.

"Just a little cut," he muttered good-naturedly. "Nothing deep."

"You didn't answer my question," I pointed out.

"It would be nice," she admitted, "but probably wouldn't work."

"Because you're too close to civilization?"

"I was thinking more about the vampires. You'd essentially be at their beck and call. You'd feel like prey—used at best."

"Dude, I said I'd buy her dinner."

Aster shoved Jeremy again, this time definitely meaning for him to end up on the floor. He grinned, winking at me as he righted himself again.

"Jeremy, what'd you mean about Sofia's boyfriend the other night?"

"When I said he was a purist?" He raised an eyebrow at me. "I meant he was a purist."

"She didn't hesitate when she charged the guy. What if that's because she wasn't scared? What if it's because she knew him and didn't want me to figure it out?"

"If she hesitated, you wouldn't have noticed," Jeremy said. "She's a vampire, remember?"

Fine, so vampires were fast. But I didn't care what he said—she had not hesitated. She was, however, fierce and secretive and angry. She'd also been grappling with the guy's hood. I'd thought she'd been trying to unmask him, but what if it was to protect his identity?

"Uh oh." Aster shifted in her seat as the bell rang. "I don't like that look, Grace."

I shrugged. There were a lot of things I didn't like. This, at least, was something I might be able to do something about.

At lunch, I wove through the maze of tables directly to Sofia.

Aster chirped a hello, assuming I was there for her. Jeremy winked, asking if I'd come for him to buy me dinner.

I ignored them both. "Did you know who it was, behind me?" I asked Sofia. "Did you recognize them?"

"What are you talking about?"

"Last night. You didn't hesitate. Like you weren't afraid because you knew they wouldn't hurt you."

"I'm not afraid of anything," she snapped.

"Was it your boyfriend? Were you fighting about all this purist stuff?"

"You think I'd be arguing with him about that? You don't think I'd be right there at his side?"

"Maybe you were." I tossed the crumpled flyer I'd stuck in my pocket that morning onto the table. "Maybe you are."

She waved a hand in the air, like it didn't matter. Like none of it mattered. Like taking someone's future in your hands and determining it for them was no big deal. Then Stella had a hand on my elbow and was pulling me to our table.

I swung around to her soft blonde hair and her soft lips and her soft nose and wanted to ask her why all the hardness around here didn't bother her. Why did it only bother me?

"How come no one's talking about these flyers?" I hissed.

"They are," she said, directing a burst of charm at me. This time it was lighter; this time it felt like a deep inhale, like spring air, like the rolling, reassuring sound of waves on the beach. "Ethan was just saying that his uncle is canvassing neighborhoods and talking to everyone who's ever said anything remotely purist. They're checking social media and computers."

I slumped down in my seat between Riah and Christian.

"No more cavorting in the woods," Christian was saying. "That's for sure."

"At least I was with her, when we were cavorting." Riah's face was innocent as he popped a raw meatball in his mouth.

Christian stiffened.

Riah offered him a tight smile. "Your word choice."

"This is the last thing I need right now," I told them both. Stella gave me a look and tossed what felt like a blanket of charm over all of us. Ethan handed her a bottle of water, which she downed in about three seconds.

Shifting in my seat, I faced Riah. "If someone from town is behind all of this, then you were right."

"About what?" Christian asked.

"About a wolf hunting here during the October full moon."

"Of course I was right." Riah tapped his nose. "I don't doubt your brain, do I?"

"Probably the same wolf I saw last night. He and his vampire friend must be responsible for the fliers."

Christian tugged at my sleeve. "That wolf…"

That wolf and his dream. I knew.

Stella looked from me to Ethan. "Let's talk about something else."

He took the bait. "How about my little wooden box?"

She rolled her eyes to me. I smiled. "Yes. Let's talk about something harmless."

"Okay, fine," she said. "What's in the little wooden box?"

I made a big show of thinking, since Riah and Christian were both disgruntled and would definitely not play along without some prodding. Riah couldn't get over how careless Christian had been letting me walk into the woods, and Christian was likely still stuck on the word "cavorting."

"What about a contract from when they started Shady Woods," I said. "Is there such a thing?"

"Yes," Christian replied. "It's under glass in town hall."

Taking a bite out of my sandwich, I considered this. "Okay, forget about the little wooden box. What's the town's origin story?"

"Our great, great grandparents founded it ninety some years ago." Christian squeezed one eye shut while calculating this again in his head, then nodded in confirmation. "And when I say our, I mean mine and Ethan's, mainly."

Riah snorted.

Ethan spun Stella's third water bottle on the table. "It started before that, some small, underground community. My dad was the only vampire. His second wife let him drink from her so he'd been able to mainstream."

"My grandparent's grandparents bought a summer camp on the lake, so everyone could escape the city and not worry about the normals." Christian reached for my hand and slid his fingers through mine. "That's all that was here at first."

Stella snatched up her water bottle from beneath Ethan's fingers and uncapped it. "The sirens were literally able to spend months at a time in the water, instead of sleeping in their bathtubs. They were the first to stay year round."

"When the blood bank opened, my dad searched out some old friends he thought might appreciate not living on the streets." Ethan leaned back in his seat. "He says if anyone remembered what hiding was like, they wouldn't be entertaining any of this purist baloney. That the best a purist can hope for is the fringes and 'gutters' of society, both awful choices."

"He's lived them both?"

Ethan nodded.

"And now there's a campaign to upend it all." Riah balled his soda can into a small chunk, letting it fall out of his fist with a clunk. "Effectively ruining my cavorting."

"Riah."

He looked at me defiantly.

Why are you needling him?

"You shouldn't have been out there," Riah muttered.

Christian growled. "You don't think I know she shouldn't have been out there?"

Knock it off, would you?

Riah's expression softened with a sigh.

"Let's make a plan for the next full moon," Stella said brightly.

"I'm sorry." Riah said it to me, but I let Christian think it was for him.

Christian nodded. "I appreciate that."

Riah opened his mouth. I kicked him under the table, and he shut it.

"The four of us should go to dinner," Ethan suggested. To Riah, he mouthed, *not you.*

"I've been wanting to take Grace to the Bluegill's Perch," Christian said.

Riah snorted. "I hate that place. There's no meat on their menu."

Stella clapped her hands together. "Perfect. I love The Bluegill's Perch."

"Now,"—Ethan winked at me—"back to the little wooden box."

Chapter 10

This Was My Life Now

Our lives now felt particularly punctuated by the full moon. There'd been no luck finding the two men who'd attacked me the night of the festival, and waiting for the full moon felt like waiting for them to expose themselves.

We had an uneventful evening at The Bluegill's Perch, and I was home safe before the sky even turned to ink. Our Saturday morning breakfast was also peaceful. No news, my dad said, was good news.

Normally, after breakfast, Riah would stop by and get me on his way to Ethan's, or Christian would show up and we'd watch endless episodes of whatever medical drama we could find that we hadn't already seen. Since last night had been the full moon, however, Riah wouldn't be home anytime soon and Christian had slept in Iara. Whenever he slept there, he slept longer.

Antsy, I brought Zeus for a walk. He led me straight for Riah's neighborhood, like he had some sort of homing device for him, even when he wasn't in town.

When we took our first turn, Zeus tugged toward a small animal carcass at the curb. It was completely picked apart.

With a shiver, I zipped up my jacket and asked Zeus to keep moving rather than investigate the dead animal. Not now and not ever.

The next street over, there were two more. Piles of bones, really, like the discards of a chicken wing meal. I stopped dead in my tracks because that was exactly it. They were remnants of werewolf meals.

I took my phone out and sent a picture to my dad, then Riah, Aster, and Christian.

Turning onto Riah's street, at the stretch of woods before the houses picked up again, I spotted another, big enough to be a deer. Roughly the size of a human.

No, it wasn't a human.

Zeus sat down next to me when I stopped this time. He looked up, as if wondering what we were going to do.

Unable to bring myself any closer to it, I zoomed in for another picture to send to my dad and Riah. Most of the roadkill I'd ever seen had been old—dark and rotting. This was fresh and bright, so now I knew werewolves didn't drink blood. The puddle soaked into the cement beneath the deer implied that at least. Skin and bones, that's what was left. Skin and bones and blood.

My stomach did not feel so good. Probably should have listened to my parents and gone a little easier on the bacon.

A barrage of dings came from my phone. First, a text from my dad: **Sending Justin to pick you up.**

Then Riah: **What in the ever-loving %$#&?**

Christian was next: **I'm coming over.**

And Aster: **You were locked up, right?**

Nope, I replied. **Texting you from the gutter. Don't have much time left. Will miss**

I purposely stopped there and hit send.

Not funny, Grace.

I knew that. If it was funny, my stomach might not be swishing so much.

I told myself not to look into the woods, but my imagination filled it in anyway. Dead animals hanging from branches and laid out over bushes like that melting clocks painting, only bloody carcasses and a forest instead of clocks and a desert.

Justin pulled up, and Zeus leapt into the truck. "I'm not in any danger," I said. It was clearly from the full moon, and that was over. All wolf fangs and claws retracted with the first vestiges of early morning light. No matter that they weren't supposed to do that here.

Riah was right. What in the actual—

"Grace. Get in the truck."

I fumbled with the door and held my hands tight in my lap as we drove the short way home. I held them so they wouldn't shake and tried to tell myself that the rest of me wasn't shaking either.

Zeus and I sat on the front porch to wait for Christian. I held my stomach in my hands and took deep breaths to steady myself. The crisp scent of fall, that's what I got, not dead bodies. No dead bodies on my street.

Wondering what those smaller animals might have been, I was searching 'wild animals of northern Wisconsin' when Christian drove up.

Red fox, probably. Or bobcat.

"Hey, hey." Hurrying the last few feet to me, he crouched down in front of where I was propped on the steps and wiped the tears I didn't realize were falling down my cheeks. "Did something happen to Riah?"

"How could anything happen to Riah?" I held my phone up. "Here I am, thinking they're just...just...not so bad. Then this happens, as if to prove to me they're monsters. As if to prove how stupid I am, and how I still don't get it. How I'll never get it. This town..."

He took my face and wiped my eyes and kissed my cheeks and then sat down next to me and wrapped my hand in his. I choked on the fact that I'd just said out loud what Riah, all this time, had been afraid of me realizing—that he was a monster.

But he wasn't a monster. He was quite possibly the kindest, most loyal, gentlest friend I'd ever had. I folded over and squeezed my eyes shut, trying to get rid of the images. The ones I made up more than anything, the ones of melty corpses in the forest.

How many animals would one wolf eat in a night? I wondered.

"Less than what are on the streets this morning," he replied, as cautiously as I'd ever heard him.

"So it's not just one wolf and one vampire anymore."

Wrapping his arm around me, he shook his head. "But that doesn't mean Riah is a monster."

"Thank you for sticking up for him." *For once.* But still, the ripped up skin, the piles of bones and fur, the lifeless eyeballs on nearly detached heads, the entire haunted-Halloween-town of it...

I wrapped my arms around my knees, and Christian un-wrapped himself from around me to rub my back. At least I wasn't crying anymore. "No matter how many times Riah told me... I thought, they're just animals, doing animal things. They what, come up to my waist, maybe? How terrible could they be? They don't have opposable thumbs; they can't hold a gun." I looked over at him. "I know deer are prey animals anyway, but... I'm a deer. How would I protect myself from that?"

"You lock your doors, that's how."

"Who do you think it was? How many?"

He tucked a piece of hair behind my ear. "We'll have answers soon."

"What do you mean?" I pulled away a little to get a better look at him.

"Someone was bit by a wolf last night. A girl from our school with dark hair like yours. My dad left me a note." He shook his head. "Anyway, I knew you were safe, that you weren't one of the victims at the clinic."

"Victims?" I echoed.

"Two more vampire bites, the wolf bite, and the wolf who did the biting. Happened right outside Parrino's. Ethan's dad saw the whole thing, stepped out of his restaurant and shot the wolf in his leg. Blew it up really."

I stared at him. "What if that had been Aster's leg?" Or Riah's. Any of our friends, who left carcasses littered behind them. And how could I feel so conflicted about this—worried for how it could have been them, and at the same time thoroughly terrified of what they could do?

Christian studied me carefully. "There'd have been no other way to stop it, unless it had been his head."

If I woke up every full moon to carcasses on the streets, would I choose to live abnormal the rest of my life? One morning a month. One night locking myself away. It had sounded like a good compromise before seeing the reality of it played out.

If I was bit and became one of them, could I live with myself? I still planned on going to college with Charlie. I still planned on becoming a nurse. I could see how I might end up back in Shady, mentoring under Christian's dad, but that wasn't a sure thing. Unless it was a forced thing.

We all knew how I didn't like to be forced into anything.

"I want to learn how to defend myself." This was my life now. I needed to be prepared. "I need to be able to kill someone if I have to."

Christian choked on that a little.

"The vampires, who already know how to kill someone, are learning how to fight right now in skills. Why aren't we?"

"We will, eventually. We just have to work up to using that much brain power."

"I don't have time to work up to it. What if Sofia isn't there to save me next time?"

Both of our lips twitched at this absurdity.

"Vampires can kill people, werewolves can kill people, sirens can probably charm people to death, but we have to wait?" I snapped my fingers. "I'll be right back." Running up to my room for the dictionary of tear formulas he'd bought me, I brought it back and handed it to him. It wasn't written in English. "There's got to be a recipe for a poison in here."

He flipped it open to the appendix and scanned the page. "Grace, even if there's a poison, what are you going to do? You know how these things work. You have to use them fresh or they lose potency."

"Fine. What kind of self-defense do you know?"

"My self-defense ends at my dendrite blood being contaminated with siren blood. And as far as the electricity we'll eventually have at our fingertips, like I said, that can't be rushed."

"So I'm going to need Riah for this?"

He frowned. "How about Ethan, or Aster."

Chapter 11

But You Want It Open?

Ethan told me his self-defense consisted of natural speed and sharp teeth. Aster said, "Sure, I could teach you a few moves."

She came over on Sunday, dressed me in leggings, a sports bra, and a sweatshirt to match her, then directed us out to the chilly November backyard. Zeus settled in a sunny spot on the grass.

"Eyes, nose, throat, and groin, okay?" She pulled her hair back into a pony. "That's what I want you to remember. In fact, I want you to recite it every morning and every night while you brush your teeth."

I nodded. "Eyes, nose, throat, and groin."

"Say it again. And put your hair up."

"Eyes, nose, throat, and groin." I wound my hair into a messy bun with the band I had on my wrist.

"Those are the most sensitive parts of the body. Do not forget them."

"Even on a wolf and vampire?"

"Even on a wolf and vampire."

"What if they come up behind me?"

"Use your elbows. They're the pointiest, hardest bits about you. Or shove your keys over your shoulder into their eyeball. Make sure you hold them like this, with your longest key between these two fingers." She stuck her thumb between her pointer and middle finger. "If you're alone, or anytime you're out walking right now, hold your keys in your hand like this. Always prepared."

"Okay, but a key isn't going to kill anyone."

She put her hands on her hips. The breeze blew her hair over her shoulder. "You can't kill anyone with your bare hands unless you're a werewolf."

"What would you do if you're a werewolf?"

"Probably rip their throat out."

I nodded. "I seem to remember Riah mentioning how you all do that, as a thing."

"We don't do it as a thing, it's just... It doesn't matter. You're not strong enough."

"Right." I squinted at her. "This is pointless, isn't it?"

"Not pointless. You sink that key into my eyeball, or knee a male wolf hard enough in the groin, and you'll have time to get away."

Then she had me practice nut shots for an hour until I was stable enough that she didn't think the wind would blow me over.

"Great! Good job!" But her praise was oddly condescending. "Now do that every morning and night after brushing your teeth. Eyes, nose, throat, groin, and kick."

"You seem to really be enjoying this." I held my sweatshirt out to get some crisp November air against my sweaty skin.

"Oh! If you have a good angle, especially if you already kicked them in the nuts and they're doubled over a bit, you could add an open palm to an ear. That's really disorienting."

Dropping my sweatshirt, I studied her. "You know that first-hand?"

"Yeah, bears do it. I don't think they mean to, they just swing sideways." She brought her arm out wide and made the motion. "Plus, no fists, you know?"

"But, you're a wolf when you fight bears."

"Still have ears." Fingering through the hair behind her ear, she stepped forward to show me a scar. "See? That's where his claws grazed me." And she was proud of it.

Riah had mentioned bears a few times too.

"Wanna see the rest of them?" she asked, whipping off her sweatshirt before I had time to answer.

The blood sort of rushed to my head as she twirled in front of me, as I took in the puckered flesh on her hip and the long, raised hook on her side. Other little ones, here and there, and on the cusp of her shoulder I'd never noticed before. It was scary, even now, after the fact, in my backyard, in the middle of the day, sun shining brightly, the breeze decided on winter. I'd worried for them, then stared at those carcasses and decided they were in fact the dangerous monsters of the world, but here I was once again reminded how vulnerable they were, how easy it might be to lose them to a hunting injury.

I swallowed hard. "Aster."

"Cool, right?"

"No."

She stared at me, then frowned. Maybe the first real frown I'd seen on her. "It has to be cool, Grace, because it's life. If it wasn't cool, if it didn't make me awesome, it would be mildly horrifying."

She dropped her sweatshirt back over her head and I gaped at her, because it *was* mildly horrifying.

"Stop it. Stop worrying right this instant. It's completely normal, and we all survive."

Except her brother hadn't survived.

I rushed across the grass to Ethan's, hopping the chain link fence and knocking once on their back door. Bursting in before anyone answered, I headed straight down to the basement, past Ethan and Stella making out on the couch.

Riah was on his phone, texting 'Addy.'

Whatever. "Let me see your scars."

He glanced behind me to where Aster stood. "You showed her your scars?"

The way he said it, like they all had them... My heart rose higher in my throat. "Let me see," I demanded, my tone the only sure and solid piece of me at the moment.

He cleared his throat and shook his head the slightest bit.

"I think that very imperceptible head shake means he doesn't have any," Aster said.

"Show me!" I snapped. It startled Ethan and Stella enough to pull them apart.

There were a few moments of silence before Riah stood and lifted his shirt. Clearly fleshed out claw marks ran down his side, disappearing under the waistband of his pants. My jaw dropped. I hadn't noticed them last summer, swimming at Stella's, so they must have been recent. He'd recently been gored in the side. Split open. How long had it taken to heal? Where had I been?

Glancing to his face and back, I teared up. Sinking onto the couch, I wiped at my eyes. "You should stop scratching yourself," I muttered, because there were also marks on his stomach from him having just done that.

"Way to go, As."

She smacked him. "Don't call me that."

"You smell her now? That's on you."

"A little worry never hurt anybody."

Settling against me in his spot on the couch, Riah nudged me, as if that was all he had to offer in the way of reassurance.

"This is cool." Picking up the little wooden box with one hand, Aster itched herself with the other. "What's in it?"

"Probably just someone's lunch," Riah said.

"Can wolves be allergic to dogs?" I asked. Zeus was right next to Aster, but Riah had been scratching before we got here. Maybe there was enough dog hair collected on the couch...

"Only silver," Ethan replied.

Stella gasped. "It's full of silver! A big hunk of silver! Or molten silver. Or pebbles of silver. Shake it. What's it sound like?"

"I don't understand this game." Aster scratched her arm in unison with Riah, who was scratching his chest, his hand snaking up under his shirt. "What's in it, for real?"

"We don't know," I told her.

"Ethan's been trying to get it open for like six months," Stella added.

"Really?"

"Literally forever," he said. "I'm about to drill a hole in it."

"I told you," Riah growled. "You're not drilling a hole in it. You're not breaking it. It's beautiful. Have some respect."

Aster stared at Ethan. "But you want it open?"

"Of course I want it open."

So just like that, Aster popped the lid from the base with her werewolf strength, the lock and clasps busting like crackers.

She dropped the box, almost recoiling from it, and whatever was inside tumbled under the couch. Folding over, her hands hit her knees, but even one of them seemed to buckle. Riah too, collapsed into himself. As if their bodies were being forced to a center.

Aster reached for Riah's shoulder. Before she could touch down on it, though, they both tore up the stairs like they were running for a bathroom and going to be sick.

Ethan scrambled across the coffee table and onto the floor, arm bending at an odd angle to reach beneath the couch for whatever had fallen out of the box. Settling back on his knees, he frowned. "It's just a rock."

I stared at it, and at the box lined on the inside with what very well could be silver, then took to the stairs, flew through the house, and stopped on the porch. Across the street and more than a few houses down, Riah was panting, hands on his knees. Aster was splayed out on the curb like a giant had dropped her there, not unlike the werewolves had dropped the carcasses. Ethan and Stella tumbled out of the door behind me, while Zeus sprinted past us all, slowing once he reached Riah.

I started walking, then sped up to a run, stopping when I was still maybe five feet from them.

Aster put her hand up to the sky. "Do you have it on you?"

"Still in the basement," Ethan said from behind me. "Back in the box as best it can be." Because she'd busted it.

Riah was trembling now. I slid a hand over his shoulder to absorb some of it. "What's going on?"

"The itching, all this time… Oh, God." He dropped down next to Aster on the curb, out of my reach. "What if we'd attacked you?"

"It's moon stone in that box," Aster said, righting herself to a sitting position.

Riah pulled his head up with seemingly great effort. "Actual rock from the actual moon."

Ethan took a great intake of air at this revelation. "Brilliant."

"Not brilliant," Riah clipped.

"It will turn a werewolf at any time," Aster said, leaning into Riah and letting him lean into her. "Bury it ten feet deep."

Stella, who'd approached in time to hear that, headed back to the house.

"Grace." Riah hung his head. "You were right next to me."

I squatted down in front of him. "It's over. I'm in one piece. You are too."

"Hey." Aster elbowed him. "Maybe this was what Christian's dream was about."

Riah clutched his fingers tight in his hair. "What if we'd killed her?"

"We didn't." She took his face in her hands and said again, sternly, "We didn't."

"Your wolf isn't you," I reminded him.

"It is, though," he muttered, as Aster let go of him. "That's precisely the problem."

Aster and I shared a look. I sank down next to him and leaned against him, but he stiffened.

"You're not going to hurt me." I knew that was true. He would do anything in his power not to hurt me. Aster too. Maybe they were vicious creatures when the moon was full, but they did everything they could to make sure they protected the world from themselves. Less could be said for plenty of humans.

Maybe it was part of the reason werewolves were so loyal, honest, and true by nature, to make up for it.

Stella called from the porch that she couldn't find a shovel in the shed, and Ethan muttered, "Right. Burying. Pronto."

"What in the world would be the point to wielding a moon rock?" Aster asked. "Turn a wolf like that and wouldn't they just turn on you?"

"Unless wolves have more control than you give yourselves credit for."

They both ignored me. "Where's it from?" Aster asked. "Where'd you find it?"

"The park," Riah answered. "Just sitting there, off the path, at the park."

"Who would lose something like that?"

"Do you think it was left on purpose?" I leaned forward to look at both of them, to see Aster better around Riah.

Aster looked at me. "Why, though? In the hopes that someone would find it, a wolf would turn, and chaos ensue?"

"Yes," I admitted. It was the only thing that made sense, if it wasn't lost. "If you were a purist..." I slid my arm through Riah's but the contact only made him stiffen again. "Stop it," I whispered. *Do I smell horrified by you?*

"No, but I'm horrified," he hissed. "Come to think of it, why aren't you horrified?"

"I'm not gonna lie, that morning after the full moon, I was." But the point was how I felt about him now. How I felt about them both. Setting my head against his, I closed my eyes and brought up as much of Riah as I could. My gut's reaction to seeing him, how my heart held him, what my mind believed of him. It spun and mixed together until it was one thing, until I could hold it, control it, and send it.

I opened my eyes and straightened a bit. He looked over at me in surprise.

I smiled. There wasn't much like feeling for yourself how someone felt about you. Christian got me with it every time. "I thought you could smell it anyway."

"Sort of. It's hard to sort through when it's someone you..." He swallowed. "Do it again."

This time I didn't close my eyes but held his gaze. I tried to bring up more: our history, inside jokes, all the little memories that made us best friends. How he warmed me and how safe he made me feel, how much fun we had together and why I thought he was amazing, even and including how he handled the full moon. Because I wasn't any better, really, not unless I planned to go vegetarian or he ever ate a human.

Somehow I trusted that he wouldn't though, even if he was a wolf. Somehow I trusted that he'd be able to stop himself.

I sent that trust first, then the faith, the love, and maybe there was a little adoration. Fine. I guess he knew now. Whatever, he needed it more than I did. It worked too. As it settled onto his senses, he finally relaxed into me.

"Okay," Aster interrupted. "I don't know what you two are doing, but can I get some?"

I grinned, reaching my arms around and past Riah to grab her closer and hug them both. Aster did the same from his other side, and we squeezed harder to reach each other until Riah groaned. "You guys are suffocating me."

"I feel like that's a challenge." Aster smirked. "And I accept."

Chapter 12

Why's She All Over You?

The five of us decided not to tell anyone about the moon rock, figuring it was safer hiding deep in Ethan's backyard than anyone else knowing it existed. Buried, at least, it couldn't do any harm.

Unfortunately, Christian's dream had not dissipated with the girl from our school getting bit, so we were back on that train. He chattered nonsense all the way to school Monday morning, one hand on the wheel, the other on the crystal that hung around his neck. It had become a barometer for how anxious he was. Tucked beneath his shirt, his panic was under control; resting over, I knew he'd had his hands on it—*needed* his hands on it.

It was a relief to finally sit down in class and think of concrete things. I opened my textbook to the chapter on dendrite history.

We'd evolved more naturally, like the siren, as opposed to a spider bite and a genetic abnormality.

Wolves, not unlike the genetic abnormality of the white tiger, could be traced back to one person—or in the tiger's case, one tiger. I'd been in awe of this for weeks. The human race is trekking along, doing its reproductive thing, when a special gene slips its way in there and throws a kink in things, creating a whole new species.

Siamese cats and Himalayan rabbits were also the result of a genetic abnormality. All of these animals had some enzyme that made them nearly colorless; they were white, with black markings most often on their extremities. I'd confirmed with Aster that werewolf fur also came in only black and white. And mottled, she'd pointed out, but never striped.

As Mrs. Smith droned on, I paged forward in the dendrite history chapter and found some fairly gruesome pictures of the witch trials. Normals had burned us at the stake and eaten sirens as a delicacy. Vampires and werewolves might have a deep, primal instinct that threatened the ones around them, but humans chose to threaten the ones around them on a regular basis. Again and again in history, humans took sides and mercilessly destroyed their enemies.

Add that to the reality of the food chain and the meat I ingested on a regular basis, and I was over the horror of my werewolf friends.

Forty minutes and five pages later, I decided to skip my locker and hold off on feeling Christian's nerves for a bit longer. I met up with Riah when I was nearly to my next class, just as Addison came at him from the other side.

"Hi, Riah. Grace." She towered over me now; she towered over both of us. "I just wanted to make sure we were still on for tonight."

"Sure, of course."

She beamed, then seemed to realize that was maybe too much and bit at her lip to contain herself. "Great. See you then."

Riah grabbed my elbow and veered us into our classroom.

I blinked at him a few times, worked my jaw like I was going to say something, narrowed my eyes at his subsequent smirk, and decided to assume he wasn't going on a first date and hadn't told his best friend.

"What?" he asked.

"Nothing."

"Liar." Right. Because he could smell me.

I followed him down the aisle. "Then why'd you ask?"

"Sometimes I want to hear you say it." He sat, stretching his legs out so I had to step over them.

"Say what?"

"That you're jealous."

"I'm not jealous!" I squirmed as I settled in my seat. "I'm trying to figure why it's okay for you to not tell me about your love life, when you positively strung the deep, dark secrets of mine out of me."

"She asked me to help her study for history."

"Why? You sleep through history."

He threw me a lazy smile. "Only because I'm already so good at it."

"Humph." I crossed my arms as the bell rang. *You realize she wants it to be a date, right?*

He shrugged and, for once, put all his attention on the teacher.

⸺ꝑꝑ⸺

At lunch, a girl slid into the chair next to Riah. A girl who wasn't Addy.

"You guys know Kiara?" he asked.

"Hi." She threw out a little wave that matched her small voice, then scooted closer to him.

"Of course." Stella smiled, charm oozing. But why bother charming a siren?

Christian smiled at her too. Ethan nodded.

Riah balled a piece of raw hamburger between his thumb and forefinger and offered it to her.

Kiara's smooth, perfect, siren face twitched.

She was gorgeous, of course; sirens were. Delicate features with wide eyes, long brown hair with bangs, dangly earrings and

128

an oversized spaghetti strap dress over a white long-sleeve shirt. Ethereal because she was a siren, skewed a bit retro by choice.

"It's not that much different than raw seafood," he said. "Try it."

The table was silent as she took it from him and slowly brought it to her mouth, eyes on him the whole time. He watched her—we all did—as she slowly placed it in her mouth, slowly closed her mouth, and even more slowly chewed, her nose wrinkling up.

After swallowing, she laughed a little and folded over against his shoulder. "The texture. I don't know how I'm going to get used to it."

"As soon as the full moon hits, you won't be able to help yourself."

Ah. I glanced at Christian. She must be the one he told me about, the girl from our school who got bit on the full moon in front of Parrino's.

"Do you have any werewolves in your family?" Stella asked. "Anyone to bring you hunting for the first time?"

"No." She blew her bangs out of her eyes. "It would be easier if I could just hunt here, honestly. But I was hoping maybe Riah would take me."

I bristled. "It is a founding tenet of this town, not to hunt here." I shoved my lunch away from me. Riah fished the deli meat out of my sandwich and added it to his own raw slices.

Are you pissed because she wants to stay? Christian asked. *Or jealous she wants him to take her?*

❧

You never answered my question, Christian said as we sat down in skills.

Sometimes, unfortunately, we had all the time to talk in skills. *She shouldn't stay, of course.*

You didn't think that was a big deal before, though. You said you'd lock yourself up one night a month, no problem. He sent me a blast of suspicion. We were supposed to be sending feelings right now, not words. But then he made it personal by asking, *What are you hiding from me?*

Nothing.

Lies sound different, remember?

I ran a hand through my hair, pulling my part over even farther than it already was. I could not tell him about the moon rock. We'd promised each other. Riah hadn't even told his dad. It was safe where it was, deep in the earth of Ethan's backyard with Zeus on watch from our side of the chain link. He loved the sun in the cooler weather, and Ethan felt better knowing that if someone were able to feel it out, Zeus would start barking like a maniac.

Are you and Riah...?

I raised my eyebrows. *Aside from the fact that I would never do that to you, or anyone, Riah may as well be dating two girls.*

And you don't like it.

Of course I don't like it. He shouldn't do that to them. Which is what should have bothered me about it, I realized, but until I said it, what had actually been bothering me was that he wasn't talking to me, wasn't giving me details. I was his best friend, and I'd spilled about us that day in the woods.

Christian studied me long and hard. *You're sure that's all it is?*

Of course that's all it is. Those girls are going through something that none of us can really understand.

He watched me a beat, then relaxed a little more. *Kiara's grandparents are still at the clinic. My dad says she's been by every day after school.*

Kiara and her dendrite grandparents had been picking up a pizza, assuming it was still safe in Shady on the night of the full moon, when they were attacked by two vampires and a werewolf.

We could go see how they're doing if you want. The nurses probably have all the gossip about what the cops got out of the vampires before they were released.

It wasn't the weirdest date ever, considering we both wanted to go into the medical field and he'd already brought me with to a volunteer shift at the blood bank.

I nodded— *Yes, please*—and this made him smile.

The basement of Dr. Riley's clinic was as much a small petting zoo as anything, the animals kept for vampire medicinal purposes.

While Christian fed them and refreshed their water, I read the signs by their cages and tanks:

TORTOISE; *Tudinidae:* For partial sedation (relaxation) and cartilage issues

OTTER; *Lutrinae:* For skin lesions (dermatology issues)

CAT; *Felis Catus:* For better cooperation (contentment)

The cat's cage was empty though, and it was roaming. She rubbed her side up against the worm farm, which was squirming.

EARTHWORM; *Lumbricina:* For regrowing appendages

In the far corner, a small glass-front freezer that looked like a beverage fridge sat on the counter. It was filled with the blood of animals too large to keep, like the polar bear—*Ursus Maritimus*—for fevers or overheating (to cool down body temp).

Christian stood from working out the world's problems with the tortoise, who I think he'd called Sir Tudinidae, as the cat rubbed against his pant leg. Then we were on our way up the steps and into the clinic itself.

We checked on Kiara's grandpa first. Christian showed me how to switch out his blood drip, which was sort of similar to the machines at the blood bank. He was chatting with him, so I wandered into her grandma's room to do hers by myself.

I hoped my smile was pleasant and not laced with pity. "Feeling okay?"

"Honestly, I'm feeling younger with every drop."

I squinted at her, because it wasn't supposed to work like that.

"Not in years, just... less back pain. No arthritis. They say those vampire smoothies at the window really help all those old lady ailments, but it's nothing compared to the real thing, straight to your veins."

I remembered Jeremy last year, on our terrible awful date, talking about elitists and how we could be the solution. Maybe this was what he meant, that vampire blood could help humans as much as human blood helped vampires.

"Did that bastard get out of here today?" she asked.

"The vampire who did this to you?"

She grimaced. "I guess I shouldn't praise the blood in one breath and call him a bastard in the next."

"I won't judge." Stopping the flow on the machine, I swapped out the blood bag, reattached the drip, and started it up again. "I can't imagine how you must be feeling."

"Well, I'm not feeling like pressing charges or anything. Especially after what that wolf did to him. He got his comeuppance, the way I see it."

"I thought the wolf…" I thought the wolf attacked her granddaughter, but didn't want to say it.

"After his leg got shot off, he went for the next closest thing. You know how they get when they're injured. Really did a number on that vampire, which was good news for me, I guess."

"I thought vampires could outrun werewolves."

"Not if they're distracted with their fangs in someone's neck."

I must have made a face, or maybe she saw my body glitch, because she reached out to squeeze my hand.

"Don't worry about me, I'll be fine."

I swallowed hard. "The fliers are convincing more people purist, huh?"

"Some stupid twenty-somethings who haven't been around long enough to remember the stories about how hard we worked to get here. Why we do the things we do." She shook her head apologetically, as if she was sorry I was one of those kids who were so far from the origin story that I couldn't understand it either. "That's what happens, you know? Younger generations, so far from tragedy, they don't see how it went wrong, how we're protecting them. They think they know everything, that it could be better. They don't know we tried that already, and it wasn't. Anyway, like I said, they got what was coming to them. That poor wolf in particular, leg blown to pieces. Won't be much of a hunter anymore, and that's about the worst thing that could happen to a wolf."

"At least they confessed." That was good. "What happens now?"

"Three times and you're out, that's what the sentiment has always been."

"Three times and you're out of Shady?"

"Right."

"So because the one vampire only bit two people,"—Addison and this poor lady—"and the wolf only bit two people,"—Kiara and the vampire—"then neither of them are out yet."

"Correct."

"But if someone presses charges..."

"They'd get a fine or some jail time."

I dropped the empty blood bag in the red biohazard container. "And if they don't?"

"That's the risk we take living here, in the open. That's what it's worth to us."

Chapter 13

They Don't Care What Day It Is

It was common knowledge by the next full moon that if you wandered outside, it was at your own risk.

The sirens planned to hide out in Iara, along with anyone who had siren blood and could naturally breathe there, while the dendrites were locking themselves in their homes for the night.

My grandpa added locks to the doors and windows on the first floor, but my parents weren't taking any chances. We were spending the night in Madison, our Chicago friends driving up to meet us for the day.

As my parents checked in, I eyeballed the hotel clerk, wondering how the founders of Shady had managed to find each other—how they were able to sort out the people they met. The guy behind the counter was tall and thin, but not quite the same dimensions as your run-of-the-mill vampire. He ran his tongue along his teeth a lot, as if he was possibly hiding fangs in there, but it was also just noon. Could be we'd simply interrupted him during lunch.

As he handed over the keys, he glanced at me and raised an eyebrow, winking as my parents turned away. Being that was more of an expression than I usually got out of Ethan, even when I tried, I chalked him up as normal.

Justin unlocked our room, and I dumped my things. Opening the door that connected our parents' room to ours, I asked, "How can you tell if someone's abnormal or not?"

"You can't." My brother grunted as he threw himself on the bed.

I slid further into my parent's room. "Ethan told me how Shady Woods started, but we never found anyone like us when we were in Chicago, right?" Because maybe they had. Maybe they'd just kept it from us.

"We weren't looking," my dad said, opening the drapes.

"That was a long time ago, honey," my mom added.

"There's no known tells? Things people do to secretly communicate with each other about who they are?"

"You'd have to ask Mr. Parrino."

So as I waited for Charlie and Matteo in the lobby, I also waited for Ethan to text me back. I was antsy and not exactly sure why. Excited to see my friends, but that wasn't it. I walked the sitting area, trailing my fingertips over the couch and chairs and lamp and plant. As my fingers danced along the fireplace stones, Charlie bounded in and threw her arms around me. Her hair was almost to her waist now, and her bangs hung more than halfway down her face.

I hugged her tightly back. She smelled like home, like Matteo's mom's homemade gnocchi and the sushi restaurant on the corner of the street. Like the lavender bush, the only truly green thing in her entire little yard, and the sunshine we baked under at the park on a regular basis.

Okay, so maybe they were memories wafting about me, and not actual scents, but I took a deep breath in regardless.

She rocked me a little, then let go. "Matty's waiting in the drop off. You ready?"

"Matty?" Charlie had been dating Tomas for three months now, another of our childhood friends, and we hadn't called Matteo 'Matty' since third grade.

She shrugged. "We're tight now. He's my new you."

"Really?"

"He didn't replace you or anything, just sort of slid into your place. He lives the closest, and he, unlike you, will watch basketball with me. Anyway, he missed you the most, aside from me, so I guess we bonded over our sorrow." She put a hand to her heart, dramatically.

I frowned and she went serious.

"He didn't replace you," she said, linking arms with me. "I still miss you loads."

"I miss you too. And I know what you mean, I guess." Because Riah.

"You guys are a lot alike, actually. So logical. And he makes fun of me when I get too full of myself."

I gasped, "*You* get too full of yourself?" But what I was thinking was if Matteo was so logical, could that mean he was a dendrite?

"Yeah, yeah." The doors opened in front of us as she pulled me outside. "Are you hungry?"

Matteo was beaming from the driver's seat while Allie hung out the back window. I squealed when I caught sight of her, since I hadn't known she was coming, and rushed over for a hug. Sliding into the front seat, I threw myself at Matteo too. I hadn't seen either of them in over a year. Their faces—their real bodies versus video calls—nearly brought tears to my eyes.

Allie, Charlie, and I talked on top of each other while Matteo shushed us so he could follow his phone's GPS directions around the square. Our first destination was the sushi restaurant, because the one in our neighborhood had been our favorite take-out in eighth grade before I'd moved away.

By the time we were seated, it was mostly Allie and Charlie still talking. As they filled me in on all the life I'd missed, Matteo watched me with a small smile on his face. He looked older, and even better, and I smiled back at him. What I really wanted to do was say something in his mind, something only we could share, because, I suppose, that's what I'd gotten used to.

When the waitress walked up, something about the delicate chin and the way she held her shoulders reminded me of Kiara. I squinted at her, trying to discern if there was a twinkle in her eye.

Back to my phone, back to bugging Ethan: **Is the phrase "twinkle in your eye" a siren thing? If they're wearing contacts, can you still see some of the shine??**

"Grace," Matteo touched my hand with his fingertip. "Want me to order for you?"

Turning my phone over, I glanced up. Right. Because he knew what I ordered; it was the same every time. "Uh, sure."

Yes! But my dad says it has to be the right light. Wolves meet in restaurants. They order steak tartare or Pittsburgh rare. That's their tell. For us, he said it's how we move. They'd go to a park or wherever runners like to run and find each other there.

"Are you okay?" Charlie asked. I glanced up. The waitress was gone and they were all watching me. Matteo with that same soft look, Charlie like she was concerned, and Allie with a smirk as if I'd been texting a boy.

I stuck my tongue out at her and shoved my phone in my pocket. "Sorry. I'm sorry. Stuff's happening back home."

"Like what?" Matteo asked. "You never talk about Shady Woods."

I blinked at him. Because Shady Woods was...

Charlie laughed. "Shady Woods is boring. Grace just wants to hear about home, Matty. And everything she's missing. Tell her about that weird Angela girl."

"She wasn't weird!" he cried. The waitress swept by to drop a bowl of roasted garlic edamame on our table, and Matteo tossed one at Charlie. Charlie swatted at it, causing it to bounce onto Allie, and Allie squealed. She had an aversion to the little soybean pods because they were 'hairy.'

I sat up a little straighter. Could she be a vampire? But no. She couldn't run for the life of her. Or wouldn't. Maybe it was that she *wouldn't* run for the life of her.

"Angela liked to lick your neck." Charlie pointed a pod at him before placing her teeth around it to squeeze the soybeans into her mouth. "That's weird."

I raised an eyebrow. "Was she tall and skinny? Like really tall and really skinny? Did she barely eat?"

"What does that have anything to do with it?" Matteo asked.

Right. It didn't. Not in this world. I took a deep breath and tried to relax, which was nearly impossible with all the nervous energy buzzing in my brain. Plus my head was starting to hurt. Or, more accurately, hum. It was slightly disorienting.

Oh.

I slumped back in my seat. Maybe I didn't need Mr. Parrino to tell me what a dendrite looked like in normal world. A dendrite not using their powers was distracted, antsy, and unsettled. Like something was trapped inside and needed to get out.

Closing my eyes, I reminded myself that I used to do this all the time. Granted, that was before I'd begun using my above normal brain power in the first place, but still. My parents had managed just fine. And my brother. I could too.

I did a better job fooling them the rest of our meal, and we spent the remainder of the afternoon with our jackets tucked close around us, wandering the square. We slid into coffee shops, browsed clothing shops, and had dessert at a restaurant we chose for its bright blue sign.

It was when we were trying to find our way back to the car, when Matteo wanted to bring us through a back alley, that things got awkward again.

I stopped short at the end of it. "No."

He headed in anyway.

"Matteo, *no.*"

"Grace, this is Madison," Allie said, following him.

"Still." It was all I could get out, because I wasn't worried about what they were worried about. I was worried about abnormals, and how solely unprepared I was to protect them if we came upon one. What I wouldn't give for Riah or Aster beside me right now.

"It's not even dark," Charlie said, elbowing me. "And it's Sunday."

"God's day!" Matteo yelled back, and that's what got me moving. He was so far in, if he needed me, I wouldn't be able to do anything. Not that I even knew what I'd do.

"People who…" …wanted to sink their teeth into your neck… "They don't care what day it is."

Matteo turned and waited for me. "Did something happen to you up there?"

"If it did, I wouldn't stop and tell you the sordid story in a back alley." I brushed past him. "If we're doing this, we're hurrying."

"Safety in numbers," Allie pointed out. "Remember?"

I couldn't argue with that. Even so, I didn't relax until we were back in Matteo's car. As we neared my hotel, Allie teared up, which made Charlie blow her nose, which made me almost cry. We didn't know when we'd see each other again, and that was nothing short of awful. There was a warmth and comfort with them I wasn't sure I had back in Shady, even if it was home now. A confidence in who I was to them, who I'd been, and how I'd started. They knew me, no explanations needed and no learning new things. No monsters, either.

I was always looking over my shoulder in Shady right now, and I still had things to learn. At the same time, leaving them also brought some relief. It was hard keeping my brain trapped silent.

Is Matteo a dendrite? I asked my parents as soon as I crossed the threshold of the hotel. *Where are you? Is Allie a vampire?*

Of course not, my dad replied.

Hotel restaurant, said my mom.

When I found them, I almost melted into the seat. Letting some of that energy out of my body by using my mind to speak felt like such sweet relief. *You're sure?* I asked.

"Roll?" Justin offered, hair still wet from the hot tub. He had the whole bread basket in front of him. In fact, he was nearly hugging it.

I plucked out a roll and nibbled on it. *Today was exhausting. How come you didn't tell me how exhausting it was for you all those years?*

Remember how happy we were when we moved back? my mom asked.

Yeah.

That was relief. We'd forgotten. We'd gotten used to it. We survived.

So hiding is just surviving? I thought back to what Ethan's dad said about hiding, about how it wasn't really a life at all.

If we do it again, we'd talk like this in our home. No more pushing to be normal all the time. When you were younger, it was important so you didn't let on to anyone else, but now you'd hide it just fine.

If we do it again? I echoed, without thinking much about it. But my parents shared a look, which was never good. I set the half-eaten roll down on my plate and sat up straight. *What do you mean, if we do it again?*

We've been talking about moving back normal.

I thought Grace made sure we couldn't go back, my brother said, while my jaw was still hanging.

She made sure we couldn't go back to Chicago. We were thinking Madison.

Wait. Setting my palms to the edge of the table, I leaned forward. *Is that why we're really here?*

We didn't move to Shady to be a part of a purist community, my dad said.

I pushed back and crossed my arms. "Do we get a vote or has our life already been decided for us, *again*?"

Justin snorted. "*You* decided for us, remember?"

"And what if I do it again?" I snapped.

"You won't," my mom said, with absolute certainty. "You have control over at least that now."

But it was awful today, not being able to speak like this, keeping all that energy bottled up inside.

"Nothing's been decided yet." My mom looked at my dad. "We've been really happy with the move, happier than we thought we'd be."

"Plus, I'd have to find a job, which holds us up, and I haven't given up hope for Shady." My dad reached out to hold my mom's hand, which had been resting on the table by her silverware. "But if your mom thinks it's best for you, I'd move in a heartbeat."

"Only, I can't decide what's best for you."

I saw the kink in her armor and jumped for it. "I can't go back to what I was, when I'm something else now. I'm abnormal now, and I want to be abnormal. I can't leave my friends and wonder if they're okay or not. I can't make new friends and not feel like I have to protect them. This purist nonsense will not last forever. It can't."

"And if it does?" she asked.

"Then I want to fight to get the old Shady back. I want to be part of the solution."

She watched me for a moment before turning her attention toward my brother. "Justin?"

"I'd stay if you left," he said simply.

My dad chuckled.

"What? I'm eighteen. You can't stop me."

And the chuckle died. I stared at him. My mom clucked.

He shrugged. "I'm with Grace. It's home now. Nothing else can replace it. I'm not leaving that, and I'm not leaving Clara."

My mom squeezed her nose like she did when she was trying to keep herself from crying. "I worry about you two wherever you go. All day I worry, every day. Except this one. This day was lovely."

What if a wild or purist came for us here? What if they came for me, and you weren't there? If all I knew was what I know now, I'd be a sitting duck. Shouldn't I stay until I know everything? Until I can fight, however it is I can fight some?

My dad's brow creased, but it was my mom who erupted. *Many dendrites don't learn half of what you know. Many play around with it here and there. They never get to telelectrical output or surreptitious thought placement. So, no, I don't think you need to be as prepared as you can be. And if I think you want to stay in Shady to learn how to fight, then I'll yank you back normal so quick you won't be able to think straight.*

I stopped fidgeting. The whole table was still. That hadn't gone over as I'd planned.

"You're an idiot," Justin muttered.

"Mom. I didn't mean it like that."

"Oh, you most certainly did, Grace."

It's not like the normal world is any safer. I said it quietly this time, soft and respectful. *There are rapists and serial killers and evil people in the normal world. It's just a different ballgame.*

There was silence for a moment, but for the clinking of other people's silverware on plates and the soft music being piped in above us.

"You both prefer this ballgame?" my dad finally asked.

I nodded furiously as my brother let out a definitive "yes."

My parents looked at each other. My dad shrugged and my mom nodded and that was the end of the conversation.

For now.

Chapter 14

Sofia and I Shared a Look

Due to the 25% of werewolves—or 40%, or most of them, or all of them, depending on who you were talking to—who stayed for the December full moon, we had a special homeroom now, and small groups. Four of us, one of each abnormal, the point being for us to "grow in compassion and understanding for one another."

Little did Ms. Boll know there would be no compassion or understanding in my group, not with Sofia assigned as our vampire. Kiara was our werewolf, I was our dendrite, and a girl named Nora our siren, whose family was from Chinese waters originally. Nora announced the first day that she was an old elementary school friend of Stella's. Then she'd moved her seat closer to mine and further from Sofia's. To be fair, Sofia had been filing her nails to a point.

Mrs. Boll started every morning with a new exercise designed to get us to "open up and access our feelings." She said our goal was to make sure we "felt the reality" of the others around us, so we'd be more likely to consider them when we made decisions that might affect them.

I'm not sure if this meant the school was trying to nudge the town back pacifist or if they'd just read a book about teenagers and coping.

Every morning after the exercise, as Ms. Boll slipped off her shoes and encouraged the rest of us to get comfortable, Kiara would turn to me and ask something about Riah. His favorite food (bacon, raw), his favorite sport (camping, which he made into a sport), his favorite music (this guy who did violin covers of pop songs). Then she'd go on about how he was the perfect wolf, or how he wore his hat when he wore his hat, or how he ran his hand through his hair when he didn't.

She was ridiculous. It was the one thing Sofia and I agreed on.

"Do you think I should grow out my bangs?" Kiara asked that morning, fluffing them with her fingers. "Addy doesn't have bangs. And you don't anymore, either." She glanced over at me. "But I'm kind of attached to my bangs."

Sofia and I shared our look. One a day; it was all we allowed ourselves. "You should keep them," we both said at once.

"If you love them," I said, "who cares what Riah thinks."

"Does he not like bangs?" She asked, her hand dropping back to her side. "Is that what you're saying?"

I squinted at her. "I honestly have no idea."

Sofia, focused on her nail filing, muttered, "I'm sure he doesn't give two shits about bangs, one way or another."

"I love your bangs," Nora piped up. "They're perfect for you and your face shape." She drew a heart in the air with her fingers, either because she loved Kiara's bangs or because Kiara's face was in the shape of a heart.

Sofia's lips curled up in a curt smile. Yeah, I was alarmed with how much we seemed to agree lately. I just kept telling myself she'd saved my life, so she couldn't be all bad.

Nora tilted her delicate siren head, and her silky, shiny black hair shifted like water with it. "They make you look classic and retro, all at once."

I failed to point out how the clothes and earrings worked with the bangs, in that respect. It wasn't Nora's fault I was irritated; I shouldn't take it out on her.

Kiara straightened and turned to me, yet again. "Does Riah like retro?"

"I have no idea what Riah likes." And that was true. Since I'd moved here, I'd never seen him with a girl. Not until Addison and Kiara, and I couldn't even tell if he was encouraging them or not.

Also, was Kiara so willing to change herself for a guy because she was that kind of girl or was it because she didn't know who she was anymore, having recently turned from a siren to a were-wolf? Maybe I should try to have more patience with her.

"Why does he call Addison Addy?" Kiara asked, and Sofia let out a groan. Kiara, to her credit, ignored her.

"They grew up together or something," I said. "I don't know."

"They call her Kiki in Iara." Nora said this to me, then offered Kiara a soft smile. "Tell Riah he can call you Kiki."

"I think I'd rather be talking about our feelings," Sofia muttered, blowing at her nails and slipping the file back into her bag.

Kiara pouted. "I am talking about my feelings."

"For a stupid boy."

Nora sighed. "I had a nightmare last night. It was disturbing."

"Tell us?" I asked. Because anything was better than Kiara swooning over my best friend.

"I dreamt I was a werewolf on the full moon. I bit someone and left them screaming. Then I found another person and suddenly I was a vampire, drinking their blood. I kept going from person to person to person." Silver tears welled in her eyes, but she ground her teeth hard to keep them there. "They all either died or had these horrible, painful transformations."

"That's awful," Kiara said, reaching over to grab hold of Nora's hand.

Sofia smirked. "You didn't enjoy it, even just a little bit?"

"Of course I didn't enjoy it!" she cried. "How could you ask that?"

Sofia looked to Kiara. "You enjoyed it, didn't you? Hunting last month with your boyfriend?"

I shifted in my seat. Riah's family had ended up taking Kiara with them for the last full moon. As far as I knew, though, they weren't anything official.

Kiara looked at her hands. "I don't remember much."

"Mmmhmm."I had quickly come to realize that Sofia used this as an expression of disbelief. Like, you go on ahead and keep thinking those delusional thoughts of yours, but I know better. It was super infuriating.

"I think this is all just really screwing with me," Nora admitted.

I nodded. "I don't want to be something I'm not already."

"Exactly!"

We stared at each other a moment then, because maybe that was insensitive to say with Kiara in our group.

"Why? You think you're better than us?" Sofia's arm motion encompassed Kiara and herself.

I blinked at her. "Better isn't exactly the word I was thinking."

"Less scary," Nora added.

"Yes! Less scary."

"Mmmhmm."

"If it weren't for Riah," Kiara said, twisting her hands in her lap, "I would've drugged myself."

This didn't seem to alarm anyone but me, so assuming there was more to this than I understood, I asked for clarification, "What do you mean by that exactly?"

"For the night of the full moon. Sirens are hunters, but not like werewolves are. I was terrified going in."

"Going in." Sofia smirked. "Then you loved it."

"Wait." I held up a finger in Sofia's direction, but asked Kiara, "You can do that?"

Sofia narrowed her focus on me, and I knew what that meant. Here we go. "That would be one step in the opposite direction from where we're trying to go, Grace. That would be your comfort infringing upon werewolf rights. *Drug them*, like animals, so you can sleep at night? Every day we walk around here, pandering to you dendrites, but you can't for one night give up a little for the sake of werewolf instinct and just let them be who they are?"

I swallowed hard. "I actually don't mind being locked up for one night. I never said that."

"Then get it through your head that they like it. They need it. Just like I need blood. And maybe you fools can start to consider how we've walked on eggshells for the last hundred years in this town, curtailing our appetite to drink fresh *for you*, and traveling on the full moon *for you*. There are better options, better solutions, if you dendrites weren't so haughty about hunting and natural instinct. Maybe you should all be turned into something else so you can understand us a little better. Have some compassion." She laced the last word with a hiss.

"Compassion?" I nearly snorted. "How do you suppose it would feel if you were someone's feeding bag twice a day? Think that would feel good? Like you were doing something for your community? Think we'd all agree to it? No. So then you'd have to go to neighboring towns, to attack innocent and unsuspecting victims. Think that would go unnoticed? You're drinking our blood to keep yourselves hidden and safe, because you know those humans would come for all of us if you let the cat out of the bag. The *curtailing* is just as much for you as it is for me."

She leaned far over into the center of our circle and said, "Haughty," just as the bell rang.

⸺ℓℓ⸺

"Why don't you drug yourselves?" I asked first thing in geometry, still trying to shrug Sofia's judgmental glare off my shoulders.

Aster raised an eyebrow. "City girl pro drugs?"

"Who told you that?" Riah asked.

"If you can drug yourself for the night, why wouldn't you?" It would definitely solve the shame he carried around with him.

"It's not a sure thing," he muttered. "You drug yourself and the next thing you know you wake up and find out you killed your mom or sister."

"Your mom or sister could lock you in your room," I pointed out.

"We can jump out windows. We would jump out a window, or throw ourselves at a locked door."

I rolled my eyes to him. "Not if you're drugged even a little bit."

"Because we like it," Aster said authoritatively. "That's why. He doesn't want to say it, Grace. But that's why. We look forward to it. We can't wait. The itch gets under our skin days before, and we need it."

I blinked at her. "Need it how?"

"Need the release. If we don't get it, we're cranky. It's probably like a drug, to be honest. We don't get it and there's some nasty detox to be had. Not physically. Physically, we're okay, aside from how you might feel if you weren't able to work your body out like you're used to. But mentally, not okay."

The bell rang, and by the time we broke out into groups to work together, Riah was napping.

I poked his head with my pencil. "Time for geometry."

"Can't Aster just do it?" Because Aster was one of the few non-dendrites topping the class. Like I said, she was on top of her game, whatever game she happened to be playing. "I need some sleep."

"All these girls keeping you up late?" I teased.

Aster snorted, her pencil already flying over her paper and solving problems almost as fast as I could.

Riah's eyelids fluttered closed. "Only on the full moon."

I thought of Aster's little brother and wondered what kind of instinct a wolf might have when they were only just made a wolf. "Was it harder with her there?" I asked. "More dangerous?"

"I'm not completely lucid, you know?"

I bit my lip and studied him, looking all peaceful and sleepy and not at all like he would tear after any animal at all.

He opened his eyes. "Why do you smell like that?"

"Worry," Aster diagnosed, head still bent over her paper. "Just tell her you'll stay away from the bears. She'll never know either way. And the moose."

"Moose?" I echoed. He'd never mentioned moose.

"They aren't all that friendly." Aster chewed once on her eraser, then got back to it. "Less sharp, though."

"Wait. Are you saying moose are more dangerous than bears? And you hunt them too? What else? What else is there?"

Aster paused just long enough for them to share a look, and I did not like that.

"What else is there?" I demanded.

"Nothing," they said at once.

"Hey," Riah went so far here as to lift his head. "Don't worry about me and Kiara."

"Why's she all over you, though?"

"Aster? She digs me."

Aster threw her pencil at him, then calmly retrieved another from her pencil case.

"Kiara, I mean."

He finally sat up. "I'm not dating her, if that's what you're asking."

"Are you dating Addison?" Aster asked, glancing up at us. "Because she won't stop talking about you in history. I almost jammed a pencil into my ear this morning."

"Yeah, how come both her and Addison are throwing themselves at you?"

"As if no one would throw themselves at me?"

I nudged his toe with mine, then realized how this was a thing Christian did and felt weird about it. "You are kind of hairy." It had been a joke between us when we met, not that I even noticed anymore. His arms, to me, now seemed completely normal. Proof I'd acclimated to some extent.

"You are steady and reassuring," Aster offered, like she'd just decided. Then she went back to the homework. Her pencil paused. "What I don't get is why you'd want them, though, considering they're both a bit messed up at the moment."

He frowned. "I don't want them."

What do you want, then? I wondered. *Who?*

He only stared at me, though, and the bell rang.

Chapter 15

Choose Me

I watched out the window as the sky deepened. Nautical twi-light—I knew what that was now.

Civil twilight, nautical, then astronomical. After that, the sky went black. After that, the wolves woke to the full moon.

It was the first of January, a Monday, and we hadn't had school today but we would tomorrow, no matter how many wolves decided to stay in Shady and start pure this New Year.

My mom wanted us to believe she was reading a book at the kitchen table, but she was staring blankly at it, having not turned a page in ten minutes. My brother was drumming his fingers along the counter while texting Clara, and my grandpa was unloading an arsenal from his truck into our kitchen. My dad walked into the room with a sword slung on his hip.

"Since when do we own a sword?"

"It's a machete," he replied.

"Oh, right." I palmed my forehead. "That makes more sense."

It's for the vampires, my brother explained without looking up from his phone. *For taking their heads off.*

"I thought we were only worried about wolves tonight."

"Machetes work on anybody." My mom's voice was strained and barely there.

A hand settled on my shoulder—my dad's. "Everything will be fine, Grace."

But the crates on the kitchen table in front of me, the rifle my grandma was oiling, and the machete said otherwise.

My grandpa dumped the last crate down by the front door and double checked the locks there. "Woulda been nice if they'd have started this in the summer, rather than during one of the longer lunar cycles of the year."

"What's that?" I asked, pointing to what sort of resembled a huge needle.

"It's for pressed garlic," my grandma answered. If I didn't look at her straight on, I could almost convince myself she was drying dishes. "Jab it in, and it does the rest."

"The vampires aren't going to be out tonight. Why would the vampires be out?" They'd be running more than feeding if they bothered to start pure at the same time as the wolves.

"I brought everything I had," Grandpa said. "Didn't sort it. Would you like to do the honors?" He began unpacking the crates. "Maybe we split it up, half and half. Keep some here and some at our place. All the wolf weapons should stay here, though. We'll stay with you every full moon until you move."

"Until we move?" My attention snapped to my mother.

"We'll see how tonight goes." Her voice was as steely as my glare.

My brother finally looked up from his phone with a frown. That was when it occurred to me that I should say good night to Christian. He would soon be unreachable, if he wasn't already.

You safe yet? It was a dumb question, because if he was, he wouldn't answer.

About to head down. You?

Locks are locked and weapons are had. I'd sent him pictures and emojis when it had all started.

Good night, he said.

Sleep tight, I responded, an old rhyme from our childhoods we often recited before we got off the phone at night.

Don't let the spiders bite.

If they do...

Take your shoe...

And hit them till they're black and blue.

Charlie had always argued with me that it was bed bugs, not spiders. Then my mom explained that our version was the Shady version, and we were talking Vampehr spiders. Charlie's version was "Good night, sleep tight, don't let the bedbugs bite. Wake up in the morn at the sound of the horn—smile so bright."

I love you, Grace.

I blinked at the screen. It was the first time he'd said it. Flat out, anyway. He'd implied. He was really good at implying. *I love you too,* I whispered in my head. But he couldn't hear me where he was, and before I could type it out, Zeus was barking like a fiend at the back door.

My mom looked at me sharply. "You better let him out before it's too late."

"He was just out."

Zeus appeared in the kitchen. Barked. Ran back to the door.

"You're fine!" I called.

"He's not fine." My dad stopped his pacing to check the sky out the front window. "And we have less than an hour to go."

With my phone in my hand, I headed down the hall to let him out. He charged across the backyard and vaulted himself over the four-foot chain link fence, which I didn't know he could do. I stepped outside to call him back but the words hung in my throat when I saw what he was after.

Two wilds. A vampire and a werewolf.

Zeus threw himself at the wolf in the same way he'd thrown himself over the fence. The werewolf caught him by the neck and snapped it with one hand.

Zeus' body fell, limp, to the ground, and my knees hit the cement beneath me. Tears welled in my eyes so immediately it seemed almost a reflex. The werewolf pointed, still with human fingers, to the corner of Ethan's yard where the little wooden box was buried.

Ethan, I choked. The vampire was the same one from the park last year, when Charlie was here... He had the same cloak, at

least. Had Samuel been his name? If he was looking for the box…
Ethan! I cried. *Dad!*

They both came at once. Ethan's screen door flung open at the same time my dad appeared behind me.

"Get out of my yard," Ethan called from his back stoop. My dad tried to pull me up to my feet and back into the house.

"We're only here for my treasure," Samuel replied.

The werewolf kicked at the snow until a patch of ground was cleared, then crouched down to dig with his extra-strong fingers.

If it was Samuel's little wooden box, that meant it wasn't connected to anyone in town. And if it wasn't connected to anyone in town, that meant it also wasn't connected to the town's purist movement. And if it wasn't connected to the purist movement, then what did Samuel want with it?

"Get out of my yard," Ethan repeated, this time more sure of himself.

"We left town graciously when asked and waited a good while to return. You'll be rid of us again soon, don't worry." Samuel glanced over at me. "Though perhaps, had we finished those normals off that night, things would have worked out better for you."

"How do you know how it worked out for us?" Ethan asked.

My dad had gotten me on my feet now, but I was resisting going inside.

Samuel turned back to Ethan. "I have friends."

"Are you behind the purists then?" Ethan asked. "The wolves staying to hunt?"

"I'm an elitist, if anything. Wait... Your wolves are hunting here?"

"Better get ready to run."

Nice, I told him. Samuel narrowed his eyes in my direction like he'd heard it too. But he couldn't have. I was in control of my mind now.

In a flash, he stood in front of me, cocking his head curiously. "Wilds should not have to answer to a community of which they are not a part."

My dad grabbed for my waist but before he yanked me back, my instinct kicked in. I flung my arm out, palm flat like Aster had told me, and smacked Samuel against the ear. His mouth dropped open, fangs clicking down almost as if it were a reflex, like my tears had been.

Then my dad had us inside the house. He kicked past me to shut the door, but it flung back open and the werewolf barged in. "No one touches Samuel like that."

"No one kills my dog!" I cried. That had been my Zeus. I nearly folded over in grief again, but could sense the rest of my family behind us now, which bolstered me.

My dad took a measured step up next to me and put an arm out across my stomach.

Get back and stay quiet, he instructed.

The werewolf eyed my dad's machete with a growl. Samuel put his hand on the werewolf's shoulder. "They fear us is all. You must smell her terror."

Of course I smelled of terror. This werewolf had snapped my dog's neck like it was a granola bar. His biceps bulged out of his torn sweater, and his thigh muscles were well defined under his faded jeans. Plus, he was in my house, and the sky would soon be black.

My mom clutched me from behind, her hands on my arms to tug me back some more. My dad took another step forward, as if he were trying to casually push them out of the house. The werewolf wasn't intimidated, though. He didn't move an inch.

"You're not safe in a community of purists." Samuel glanced at each of us before settling his gaze on me. "Elitists consider dendrites as above normal, due to your abilities, but purists consider dendrites a meal, due to your blood."

Even though it was cold, his shirt was unbuttoned halfway, revealing a key that hung low around his neck. The key to the broken box. The broken box, which was in Samuel's hand. How long before the sides fell apart and it affected the werewolf behind him?

He saw my attention on it and smiled. "A time will come when you will need to choose. Choose me, and you will last. Choose this town, and you will die at the hands of chaos."

As quickly as he'd shown up on my back step, he disappeared out our back door. Not the wolf, though. The wolf doubled over.

Hair sprung up from his neck like hackles, and his neck cocked at an odd angle. He fell to all fours, and with a final snap, he was no longer human.

He bellowed at me, and I stumbled back into my mom. His teeth—there were a lot more of them than two vampire fangs—dripped with saliva. Crouching back, he readied to launch himself, and my dad took his head off with one clean slice of the machete.

The terribly wrong sound of it rang in my ears as my parents and grandparents erupted in my head.

How come he changed?

He shouldn't have changed.

It's not time yet.

How did that happen?

My dad's hands were shaking. It was the only tell that he'd just killed someone. Something. A wolf that was also a person. Then Ethan was standing at our back door.

"You better get home, son." My grandpa shuffled past us, around the blood spurting from the wolf's split neck.

Ethan stared at me with horror.

"What's wrong?" I asked in a screech. "What's happened?"

"This!" he cried. "Tonight is what happened!"

"Oh." For a moment I was calm, my hand to my chest. "I thought you were coming with more bad news."

He shook his head, wide eyes not leaving mine until my grandma shuffled him out and across the yard.

The wolf head... Riah and Aster... The possibility of dead friends... Each incoherent thought I had was laced with panic and anxiety. I was shaking so hard it seemed like nothing was still. Then my mom was around me. And my dad and brother. My grandma, after carrying Zeus inside, over the wolf and into the kitchen. And finally my grandpa, after all the locks were clicked into place.

"How could we be wrong about the twilight?" my mom whispered, as the house dipped into a deeper darkness.

"We're not," I managed to say. *It was the little wooden box.*

As we stood there, huddled together, I told them everything.

Chapter 16

We Need a Wolf

It snowed the morning after Zeus died, dropping white innocence down on the destruction of the night before, on the torn up bodies littering the street. All animals, at least that I could see from my window.

Opening it, I yanked my screen out and stuck my hand into the fat flakes, letting the cold sink into me and settle in my soul.

It was the first morning I could remember that I'd woken up without Zeus at my side.

Thank goodness my grandma thought to bring him in last night, or he'd be frozen beneath all that, if not torn to pieces himself.

The side door to the garage opened, spitting out Justin and Ethan into our backyard. They each carried two shovels, one for snow and one for digging.

I scrambled out of bed and down the stairs, past my mom again at the table with a book in her hands, threw on some boots, and rushed out of the house so quickly I didn't realize until after that there was no longer a wolf head or pool of blood in our hallway.

My dad had paced all night. I'd slept fitfully, waking often to be lulled back to sleep by the steady beat of his feet on the floor below me. I suppose he'd cleaned it up, or my grandparents had.

Forcing my way through the snow as Eric, Ethan's older brother, trudged toward Ethan and Justin from the other side, I wrapped my arms around me.

When they finished clearing the snow, Ethan stood back as if Justin should do the honors on the actual hole, but the ground wouldn't give.

"Frozen," he muttered.

Ethan grabbed the shovel and tried himself, as maniacally as I'd ever seen him.

Eric put a hand on his arm. "We need a wolf."

Ethan looked over to where the wolf had been digging into frozen ground the night before. "We could bury him where the box was."

"It's not big enough." Justin dropped the shovel he was holding. It sunk and disappeared into the snow, which was how my heart had felt the moment that wolf had snapped Zeus' neck. And every moment since when I remembered he was no longer there. Numb as the white crystals dripping around us on the trees.

"We'll wait for Riah," I muttered. "He'd want to say goodbye anyway." Pulling out my phone to text him, I headed back for the warmth of the house.

I need you, was all I said. Then, **Don't go to school. Come to my house. As soon as you can. Please.**

Why? What's wrong? he asked immediately.

I'll tell you when you get here. I couldn't give him this kind of news over the phone.

You're freaking me out, Grace.

I'm clearly in one piece, Riah. With all my fingers even. WHO ISN'T?

No one. I just need you.

Zeus had been nothing to them when we all first met, nothing but a human thing, nothing to an abnormal. I'd clung to that, to Zeus, for what he represented, even though I'd technically chosen the abnormal, time and again. Had we moved back like my mom wanted to, Zeus would still be alive.

"I'm not going to school today," I told my mom, while making her a cup of tea.

"That's fine, honey."

"Riah's on his way. We'll bury Zeus when he gets here." I bit down hard on my cheeks until the taste of blood seeped into my mouth. I wouldn't cry. I couldn't. Not until it was over and I was in my room and no one would see. I had to be strong enough to handle the realities of this life or she'd sweep me back out of it.

The old radio flipped on in the living room, and my mom left her tea and book for the noise. I followed her. My grandparents and my dad were trying to find the Shady Woods channel. This wasn't something they could put in any paper, not even veiled.

"...no deaths and no injuries from last night's situation. Census will be knocking this morning to see how many stayed. We'll update you later."

I glanced at my dad. Maybe the city wouldn't count a wild's death in their toll, or maybe my parents and grandparents had made it go away.

"In other news, there have been rumors that the purists will try to find footing on our town council in the next election. It has been forty-two years since anyone has run contested, but word is that will not be the case this coming November. Adelaide Stickman has just come from town hall, where there was an unofficial meeting this morning. Adelaide?"

Both of them spoke low, like they were in a secret attic telling us of secret things. Also, I noted, Stickman was Aster's last name.

"Thanks, Tim. The group collecting outside of town hall this morning held Start Pure in the New Year posters. They're calling for changes to our tried and true traditions here in Shady Woods, considering the last two lunar cycles have not brought any death."

I glanced at my parents, then my grandparents. All of them were watching the radio. Once more, none of them twitched with the claim that no one had died.

"I spoke to multiple folks who there to support the purists planning to officially register for the next town council election as soon as the doors open at nine."

"They can't win," I muttered.

"Oh, they can," my grandpa muttered back.

"Adelaide, what is it that these purists are hoping to accomplish if they win?"

"Sheree Hoffman wanted to reassure the public that the first thing they'll do is put a sentinel force into place to ensure a safe transition from a pacifist mentality to a purist one. She stressed that no one should worry, that all species' rights will be considered, but that pacifism is a form of denial, and that we need to better embrace each other as we are."

"Would this sentinel replace the police force?"

"No, Tim. They would be more focused on establishing firmer borders to keep wilds and Hand from entering."

"So mostly a border patrol?"

"Correct, Tim. She suspects we might attract some new members to the community if we can successfully transition to 'living out loud,' as she puts it."

"Is that a goal of theirs? To attract new citizens?"

"It did sound like it, but again, she wouldn't confirm. The sentinel's job would be to make sure the right people were kept out, but those seeking a haven would be let in."

My mom strode from the doorway to switch it off. "It's time," she said, looking at my dad. "It's time to move again."

"I'd rather slit my wrists," I said vehemently.

All of them stared at me—my grandparents, my parents, and my brother, who'd come in behind me and not yet taken his coat off.

"For Ethan to drink," I explained. "Not like the normal slit your wrists." Even after last night. It seemed the more horror I experienced here, the more determined I was to stay and force it back into the fairy tale my parents had promised me it was, back when we'd first moved. The fairy tale they told of growing up here.

"You don't slit your wrists," my mom said absently. "You do it where it's not so easy for them to get carried away and drink you dry. Somewhere the flow isn't as strong."

"I'm not going anywhere," Justin said, standing next to me now, as if we were two against four. Though, I was guessing my grandparents were on our side.

"You could die," she whimpered.

My grandma slid my mom's sleeve up to run a finger over the scar on the back of her arm. "You didn't die this night. Have faith, Anna."

"I thought that was a camping accident," I said.

"We got lost, camping. For too long. Sustenance was needed." She blinked at me, eyelids fluttering to hide her tears. "I don't know how much longer I can worry about my children like this."

My grandpa grunted. "We managed fine."

"At least wait until the election," my brother suggested. "I'll be graduated and living on my own anyway, and if the wolves hunt for the next nine months and no one gets hurt…"

My mom swallowed hard and wiped her eyes. "We killed a werewolf last night. A person. One moment longer and it could have been Grace we were cleaning up alongside him."

"They weren't from around here, though," I pointed out. "And they won't be coming back.

She looked at my dad and crossed her arms. "At least one of them won't."

Chapter 17

His As Much As Mine

Riah's dad drove up around noon, tires crunching on the snow as I stepped onto the porch.

Riah nearly fell out of the car before it stopped. Seeing him broke something inside me, whatever had been holding my grief back. I threw my arms around his neck and the sobs ripped through me.

"Who, Grace? What?" He gathered me against him. "You're killing me here."

"Zeus," I managed. "They came for the box. They broke his neck. A wolf charged me." I gulped down a sob. "My dad took his head off with a machete."

Placing his hands to my arms, he pulled back to eyeball me with a raised brow. "You were outside?"

"Inside. He came inside."

"How did he get *inside?*"

I felt the sobs pushing their way back up, because why? Because he made me feel safe enough to fall apart? I didn't know, but I wrapped my arms around his neck again and held on tight. *It was before the full moon. He turned because of the box. It was a wild, and Samuel. It was Samuel's box.*

"No one's hurt?" he asked into my hair.

I shook my head. *Only Zeus. I need you to dig his grave.*

He breathed out a heavy, shaky breath, and I held on until he said yes, until I could feel him shaking beneath me because he'd loved that dog too. It was my turn to pull back now, to wipe his tears with my thumbs, a fraction of them compared to mine, but still real.

When his cheeks were dry, I wrapped my arms around his neck one more time to make sure he was there. He was at least still there.

Aster too. I knew she was safe.

A car pulled up in the driveway. I let go of Riah, and he let go of me. Christian got out of his car and stood there, silent.

Riah rubbed at his jaw. "I'll, uh, I'll go dig that grave." He headed around the side of the house furthest from the driveway.

Zeus died, I said, but I'd already told him.

I know. I came over to see if you were okay, to comfort you. Guess you prefer Riah for that.

I just told him. He just found out. I needed him to dig the grave.

The wind whistled in the vast space between us. He was still on the far side of his car, while I was still on the front steps.

You could have texted him, like you texted me.

I needed him to dig the grave. Plus, Zeus was his as much as he was mine.

Just like you're his? As much as you're mine?

I shook my head, squinting at him a little. *Christian.*

What? I told you I loved you, you never replied, and then I come over to this? What do you expect me to think?

What would you think if it were Aster?

Why isn't it? She can dig a frozen grave as easily as Riah.

Because she didn't love Zeus like Riah did. Because Zeus wasn't hers.

Just like you're not mine.

Stop saying that. I walked over to the driveway, reaching out over the top of his car for his hand. He didn't respond. His hand didn't meet mine.

This was my dream. This feels like my dream.

Last night was your dream. The wolf my dad killed. I walked around the car and watched his gaze as I grew closer, as I stepped to him and put my forehead on his chest.

We stood like that a moment—no arms, just me with my head on his chest. Then he stepped back, got in his car, and drove back to class.

Chapter 18

Always at My Side

Hours later, when it was finished, the clumps of frozen ground piled back on top of Zeus' body beneath a soft mound of snow I'd formed with my hands, I wiped the tears from my cheeks and looked around.

It wasn't only my family outside paying respects in the deep snow, but all of Ethan's too. Even his dad. Mr. Parrino was the first to go inside. Then his wife and daughter. Then Eric, Ethan, and my grandparents.

My mom brought me a warmer coat, wrapping it over the lighter one I already had on. The sun was warm and bright, only the air harsh and cold.

When my parents and Justin were gone, when it was only Riah and I left, he reached for my hand. I held onto it, and he held onto me.

"I could feel that rock trying to get under my skin when I was in the backyard," he said. "They probably wandered through town every night, waiting for him to feel something. If they knew what they were looking for..."

Could he be building some sort of army with it? I wondered.

"He wouldn't be able to control a wolf army. That can't be it."

"He said we'd have a choice." I looked at Riah, his hair a mess coming off the full moon, coming straight here. I let go of his hand. "He said if we choose him, we'll last, but if we choose the town, we'll die at the hands of chaos."

"That's ominous." He wasn't wearing gloves, and now that his hands were free, he brought them to his mouth to blow on them.

I ran the toe of my boot in the snow, remembering my first day of school here. Lying in the cool September grass, I'd sprawled out like I was making a snow angel, Zeus at my side. He'd always been at my side.

A tear dripped down my nose. A tear for my dog, for our humanity, and for this town. That it wasn't what my parents remembered it to be, or that if it was, it wouldn't be for much longer.

Standing there, the backs of our hands barely touching, I felt suddenly both free and hardened with new resolve. The tethers to my past life and my past world were flapping loose in the wind, and my feet were now firmly planted in this new one, growing roots and ties so unbreakable that I knew if it came down to it, I'd fight for them all. For Riah and Aster and Christian and Ethan. For Stella and Kiara and even Sofia. For what Shady was meant to be.

There should be a place like what my mother remembered for us all. It wasn't something to let go of. Like Samuel with his box, or Zeus and his loyalty, that was how I felt about Shady Woods now. The way my parents had grown up was something too special to let go of.

Chaos or not, it was everything.

Hands of Chaos

Book 3 in the Shady Woods series

The Sentinels were imposing, all of them, dressed in black from head to toe. And their special issue "Take back your pride!" lanyards made them seem like they were fighting something, when they were just supposed to be keeping wayward strangers out of Shady Woods.

Though I could see the point of them, in theory, I didn't like them in practice. Three currently stood in the middle of the road, down past the blood bank. The road was cleared of snow, which was piled high on the curbs, and stray holiday decorations were still strung from the town's street lamps. From here, a block away, I could see a large stain of animal blood beneath their feet, leftover from the last full moon.

"You okay, Grace?" Riah asked, yanking me from my thoughts as my friends filed inside the Silver Subs building.

With a deep breath of the icy January air, I followed. "I don't know. Am I?"

He smirked and drew in a deep breath. His wolf ability to smell emotion was like having an inside look at me, which was frustrating only because I couldn't do the same. As a dendrite, I could speak directly into someone's mind, maybe flood them with feelings and place a thought once in a while, but I couldn't read minds or poke around in them.

I knew if Christian hadn't been there, reaching his hand back for mine, that Riah would have moved closer, not that he couldn't read me just fine from where he was. "Apprehension, mistrust, and disapproval, to name a few."

"I don't like the Sentinel," I explained.

"Justin's a Sentinel."

It felt like needle pricks, hearing my brother linked to them. He'd graduated last year and I was still reeling from his decision not to go to college, even if most of the Shady residents didn't. The town operated more on an internship and family business basis, since there were very few communities like ours where above normals—abnormals for short—chose to peacefully co-exist. Definitely none with colleges. But we'd been raised to go to college. This hadn't always been my life.

My parents had grown up in Shady, moved to Chicago for college, and raised my brother and I there until my thoughts broke into some random cashier's head. Unfortunately, this cashier was part of the Hand of Humanity and that was all it took for her to commit herself to eradicating me and my family. We escaped back here so I could better learn to control myself, and to avoid the sticky situation of having to kill her before she killed us.

Regardless of my thoughts on college, and my original assumptions that Justin and I would live normal as adults, Justin had announced that he and his girlfriend Clara were going to join the Sentinel. He was going to marry her and never leave Shady, so if he eventually wanted a degree, he'd do it online. Clara was a vampire and it was hardest for vampires who wanted a normal life to live anywhere else—hard to find a blood bank willing to regularly sell a private citizen a gallon unless you were in Shady Woods, Wisconsin.

Stella ordered the cold clam chowder, Ethan a steaming mug of warm sustenance, as he put it, and Riah requested his sub meaty and raw, no veggies or sauce.

I ordered turkey, as did Christian, my mostly dendrite, somewhat siren boyfriend.

Christian waited for our subs while the rest of us grabbed a table, but as I walked past Nehemiah's booth and caught sight of his bashed in face, I stopped right there in front of him to gawk. Not very cool of me, I know.

Everyone considered Nehemiah and his friends to be trouble, but considering the tear-your-throat-out, disregard-of-human-life trouble, you'd think a few kids who liked to skip class wouldn't be a huge problem. In the few years I'd been around, I'd never seen any other sign they'd gotten in a fight. Besides, it wasn't they who'd gotten in a fight—Preston and Reilly looked just fine.

Preston noticed me first, then Reilly. When Nehemiah finally looked up from his sandwich—werewolves were that attached to food—he grinned, even winked.

"Like what you see?" he asked. Reilly snickered. Preston looked down at his sub.

"Sorry, I just…"

"Haven't seen anyone so handsome before?"

One eye was puffy and sealed shut, the other more purple than I could have imagined a bruise to be. He had thin scabs on his forehead and chin, rug burns almost, or as if his face had been pressed into the street.

I sat down next to him, as if acting like we were friends who sat next to each other could excuse my ogling. "What happened?"

"I like to explore and the Sentinel don't take kindly to that."

"I like to explore, too," Preston said, motioning to his un-marred face. "What they don't take kindly to is his mouth."

Werewolves were the strongest of us. By a long shot. Nehemiah's knuckles, however, were perfectly neat. "Did you not defend yourself?"

"I didn't." He beamed. "Wanna kiss the bruises?"

Christian appeared, subs in hand, and cleared his throat at that. Nehemiah snickered.

"Why wouldn't you defend yourself?" I asked.

"So there was something to report to the police. Something to document."

I frowned. "That's..."

"Brilliant? Yeah, you're welcome."

Christian nudged me, nodding toward our table. I stood, not sure what else to say, how to leave it. Christian left, slid into our booth, and as I turned away, Nehemiah caught my hand.

"Grace, right?"

I nodded. He let go and got back to his sandwich.

"This is a problem," I said as I sat down. "The Sentinel are a problem."

Stella shrugged both thin shoulders, Ethan took a drink, Christian muttered how Nehemiah was the problem, and Riah slid a newspaper across the table.

A real newspaper. Because Shady news didn't make it online in case any conspiracy theorists might figure it for the truth. The headline on the front page read "We've lost sight of where we've been." It was an op-ed piece on what the new town council had been up to since November, when purists had nearly swept the election.

Purist: an abnormal who thinks we should all live by instinct. Outside of Shady Woods, this meant vampires drinking fresh from whatever human or dendrite they might come across and werewolves tearing into whatever flesh they might happen by on a full moon. Inside Shady, it started a movement to stay locked in our homes on the full moon so the wolves didn't have to travel, instead of sending them off to the wilderness each month.

The article outlined how the new council was not following all the founding tenets of Shady Woods. Riah was touchy about the whole situation because his dad was one of only two original council members left. That meant five were purists, we had Sentinel watching our borders, and Riah thought everything meant something.

I turned to Christian. "You think Nehemiah deserved that? You think anyone could deserve that?"

"I think he should keep his hands off you."

Rolling my eyes to Riah, I said it again. "The Sentinel are a problem."

"I'm more worried about Hollywood."

I snorted. "That's cute."

"No, I'm serious. Look at this." Unlocking his phone, he opened it up to a website and set it down on top of the paper. "A bunch of celebrities didn't show for the film awards."

Christian peered at it. "That's just gossip."

"It's national news. One producer made a joke about them being werewolves, because it was the full moon, but what if it's true?"

"How many of them?" I asked, always willing to go a little further down Riah's rabbit hole than the others.

"Three."

Stella turned his phone toward her and started reading, her strawberry-blonde hair falling like water around her face when she dipped her head.

"They probably just flaked." Ethan wiped a drop of blood off the edge of his mug. "They're celebrities."

"Two of them were supposed to present the lifetime achievement award. You don't bail on that unless you have to."

"It says right here Cynthia Jackson had the flu, Glinda Rae needed a mental health day, which—and I quote 'is not abnormal for her'—and JD Sanger, well, he can do pretty much whatever he wants, can't he?" Stella looked up at Riah.

"Why would this friend say"—he snatched his phone from her and scrolled back up—"JD was planning to be there. I talked to him when he was getting ready. I don't know what happened."

"Okay," I agreed. "It's fishy."

Christian rolled his eyes. He thought I humored Riah too much. Then again, he thought I everything-ed Riah too much ."If they were werewolves, they wouldn't have agreed to present on the full moon in the first place."

"Unless they didn't know they were going to be werewolves when they agreed. What if someone just turned them?"

"All of them at once?" Ethan asked.

"Three celebrities isn't really laying low," Stella agreed.

"Particularly if you know it's going to cut into the awards."

"I'm not saying whoever did it was trying to lay low."

We stared at Riah, deciding collectively without discussing it that he was taking it one step too far, then went back to our sandwiches.

Christian put an arm around me. "You sure you don't want to come to Emily's party?"

"I'm sure I'm not invited." Her birthday party was tonight. A sleepover, on a Sunday.

"But do you want to come?"

I tossed him a grin. "Not one bit." Though Aster was one of my best friends, and Jeremy and Kevin liked me enough, Sofia and Emily hated me with everything in them. The feeling was mutual, and not because Sofia was Christian's ex-girlfriend, but because they were simply awful.

"I'm not really comfortable going to a sleepover without you," he said.

"Then don't."

"We always go to each other's birthdays. It's been a thing since like second grade. Come with me."

"My parents would never let me stay over. Not on a school night. Even if I went, I'd have to be home by ten."

"Sofia and Emily have school night sleepovers all the time."

"My parents don't care what Sofia and Emily do."

"Please?"

"Never," I told him. "But I love you."

He sighed, because he felt I used those words as an apology more than anything, or to soften the delivery of something

I knew he didn't want to hear. He got out of the booth and knocked his knuckles on the table. *You always pick Riah after the full moon.*

I leveled a warning look at him. I was not going to have this conversation again. Kiara always slept for a few days after the full moon, so it was the only time I really got with Riah anymore, unless I wanted to spend time with Kiara too. Which I did not. Regardless, I wouldn't have gone to this party with him. *Riah has zero to do with it.*

I really think you should be there, Grace.

I'm not welcome, and my parents wouldn't let me. I'm going to Ethan's.

Ethan turned to nuzzle Stella, which he often did when he felt we were holding a silent conversation, one dendrite mind to another. It was rude of us, but nearly impossible not to once in a while, when you could.

Christian's lips pressed tight while he rubbed at the crystal strung around his neck—the crystal he'd bought to help him make sense of his dreams.

Did you have a dream you didn't tell me about? I asked.

He shook his head, but it seemed more like a sad, disappointed shake than an actual answer, knocked one more time on the table, then left.

Also By J Mercer

More of the Shady Woods series

Shady Woods

The Little Wooden Box

Other young adult novels

Triplicity

Perfection and Other Illusive Things

Reviews really do make the world go round. Please let others know what you thought!